28/9/20

Please return/renew this item by the
last date shown to avoid a charge.
Books may also be renewed by phone
and Internet. May not be renewed if
required by another reader.

www.libraries.barnet.gov.uk

BARNET
LONDON BOROUGH

'It is like nothing we've read before. *Nutshell* is a
gripping domestic drama'

Tracy Chevalier, *Good Housekeeping*

'The book's finest exploration is of poetry. The author offers up everything he knows about its intensity, and why he loves it so. It is clear Mr McEwan has had enormous fun writing *Nutshell;* now it is the reader's turn to be entertained too. Dark as it is, this novel is a thing of joy'
Economist

'As we read, this tight little novel – like a foetus in the womb – grows into something much grander and weightier than itself'
Spectator

'An audacious, enjoyable read'
Woman & Home

'A surprising and surprisingly funny novel'
Sunday Times

'McEwan has always been an artist in the Alfred Hitchcock vein in that what's most interesting and appealing about his work tends to come from his extreme technical mastery of his medium'
Financial Times

'His most intriguing book since *On Chesil Beach*'
John Boyne, *Irish Times*

Nutshell

IAN McEWAN

Ian McEwan is a critically acclaimed author of short stories and novels for adults, as well as *The Daydreamer*, a children's novel illustrated by Anthony Browne. His first published work, a collection of short stories, *First Love, Last Rites*, won the Somerset Maugham Award. His novels include *The Child in Time*, which won the 1987 Whitbread Novel of the Year Award, *The Cement Garden, Enduring Love, Amsterdam*, which won the 1998 Booker Prize, *Atonement, Saturday, On Chesil Beach, Solar, Sweet Tooth* and *The Children Act*.

ALSO BY IAN McEWAN

IAN McEWAN

Nutshell

VINTAGE

1 3 5 7 9 10 8 6 4 2

Vintage
20 Vauxhall Bridge Road,
London SW1V 2SA

Vintage is part of the Penguin Random House group of companies
whose addresses can be found at global.penguinrandomhouse.com.

Penguin
Random House
UK

First published in Vintage in 2017
First published in hardback by Jonathan Cape in 2016

penguin.co.uk/vintage

A CIP catalogue record for this book is available from the British Library

ISBN 9781784705114

Printed and bound by Clays Ltd, St Ives plc

Penguin Random House is committed to a sustainable future for
our business, our readers and our planet. This book is made from
Forest Stewardship Council® certified paper.

MIX
Paper from
responsible sources
FSC® C018179

To Rosie and Sophie

Oh God, I could be bounded in a nutshell and count myself a king of infinite space – were it not that I have bad dreams.

SHAKESPEARE, *Hamlet*

ONE

S o here I am, upside down in a woman. Arms patiently crossed, waiting, waiting and wondering who I'm in, what I'm in for. My eyes close nostalgically when I remember how I once drifted in my translucent body bag, floated dreamily in the bubble of my thoughts through my private ocean in slow-motion somersaults, colliding gently against the transparent bounds of my confinement, the confiding membrane that vibrated with, even as it muffled, the voices of conspirators in a vile enterprise. That was in my careless youth. Now, fully inverted, not an inch of space to myself, knees crammed against belly, my thoughts as well as my head are fully engaged. I've no choice, my ear is pressed all day and night against the bloody walls. I listen, make mental notes, and I'm troubled. I'm hearing pillow talk of deadly intent and I'm terrified by what awaits me, by what might draw me in.

I'm immersed in abstractions, and only the proliferating relations between them create the illusion of a known world. When I hear 'blue', which I've never seen, I imagine some kind of mental event that's fairly close to 'green' – which I've never seen. I count myself an innocent, unburdened by allegiances and obligations, a free spirit, despite my meagre living room. No one to contradict or reprimand me, no name or previous address, no religion, no debts, no enemies. My appointment diary, if it existed, notes only my forthcoming birthday. I am, or I was, despite what the geneticists are now saying, a blank slate. But a slippery, porous slate no schoolroom or cottage roof could find use for, a slate that writes upon itself as it grows by the day and becomes less blank. I count myself an innocent, but it seems I'm party to a plot. My mother, bless her unceasing, loudly squelching heart, seems to be involved.

Seems, Mother? No, it *is*. You are. You are involved. I've known from my beginning. Let me summon it, that moment of creation that arrived with my first concept. Long ago, many weeks ago, my neural groove closed upon itself to become my spine and my many million young neurons, busy as silkworms, spun and wove from their trailing axons the gorgeous golden fabric of my first idea, a notion so simple it partly eludes me now. Was it *me*? Too self-loving. Was it *now*? Overly dramatic. Then something antecedent to both, containing both, a single word mediated by a mental sigh or swoon of acceptance, of pure being, something like – *this*? Too precious. So, getting closer, my idea was *To be*. Or if not that, its grammatical variant, *is*. This was my aboriginal notion and here's the crux – *is*. Just that. In the spirit of *Es muss sein*. The beginning of conscious life was the end of

2

illusion, the illusion of non-being, and the eruption of the real. The triumph of realism over magic, of *is* over *seems*. My mother *is* involved in a plot, and therefore I am too, even if my role might be to foil it. Or if I, reluctant fool, come to term too late, then to avenge it.

But I don't whine in the face of good fortune. I knew from the start, when I unwrapped from its cloth of gold my gift of consciousness, that I could have arrived in a worse place in a far worse time. The generalities are already clear, against which my domestic troubles are, or should be, negligible. There's much to celebrate. I'll inherit a condition of modernity (hygiene, holidays, anaesthetics, reading lamps, oranges in winter) and inhabit a privileged corner of the planet – well-fed, plague-free western Europe. Ancient Europa, sclerotic, relatively kind, tormented by its ghosts, vulnerable to bullies, unsure of herself, destination of choice for unfortunate millions. My immediate neighbourhood will not be palmy Norway – my first choice on account of its gigantic sovereign fund and generous social provision; nor my second, Italy, on grounds of regional cuisine and sun-blessed decay; and not even my third, France, for its Pinot Noir and jaunty self-regard. Instead I'll inherit a less than united kingdom ruled by an esteemed elderly queen, where a businessman-prince, famed for his good works, his elixirs (cauliflower essence to purify the blood) and unconstitutional meddling, waits restively for his crown. This will be my home, and it will do. I might have emerged in North Korea, where succession is also uncontested but freedom and food are wanting.

How is it that I, not even young, not even born yesterday, could know so much, or know enough to be wrong about so much? I have my sources, I *listen*. My mother, Trudy, when she isn't with her friend Claude, likes the radio and prefers talk to music. Who, at the Internet's inception, would have foreseen the rise and rise of radio, or the renaissance of that archaic word, 'wireless'? I hear, above the launderette din of stomach and bowels, the news, wellspring of all bad dreams. Driven by a self-harming compulsion, I listen closely to analysis and dissent. Repeats on the hour, regular half-hourly summaries don't bore me. I even tolerate the BBC World Service and its puerile blasts of synthetic trumpets and xylophone to separate the items. In the middle of a long, quiet night I might give my mother a sharp kick. She'll wake, become insomniac, reach for the radio. Cruel sport, I know, but we are both better informed by the morning.

And she likes podcast lectures, and self-improving audio books – *Know Your Wine*, in fifteen parts, biographies of seventeenth-century playwrights, and various world classics. James Joyce's *Ulysses* sends her to sleep, even as it thrills me. When, in the early days, she inserted her earbuds, I heard clearly, so efficiently did sound waves travel through jawbone and clavicle, down through her skeletal structure, swiftly through the nourishing amniotic. Even television conveys most of its meagre utility by sound. Also, when my mother and Claude meet, they occasionally discuss the state of the world, usually in terms of lament, even as they scheme to make it worse. Lodged where I am, nothing to do but grow my body and mind, I take in everything, even the trivia – of which there is much.

For Claude is a man who prefers to repeat himself. A man of riffs. On shaking hands with a stranger – I've heard this twice – he'll say, 'Claude, as in Debussy.' How wrong he is. This is Claude as in property developer who composes nothing, invents nothing. He enjoys a thought, speaks it aloud, then later has it again, and – why not? – says it again. Vibrating the air a second time with this thought is integral to his pleasure. He knows you know he's repeating himself. What he can't know is that you don't enjoy it the way he does. This, I've learned from a Reith lecture, is what is known as a problem of reference.

Here's an example both of Claude's discourse and of how I gather information. He and my mother have arranged by telephone (I hear both sides) to meet in the evening. Discounting me, as they tend to – a candlelit dinner for two. How do I know about the lighting? Because when the hour comes and they are shown to their seats I hear my mother complain. The candles are lit at every table but ours.

There follows in sequence Claude's irritated gasp, an imperious snapping of dry fingers, the kind of obsequious murmur that emanates, so I would guess, from a waiter bent at the waist, the rasp of a lighter. It's theirs, a candlelit dinner. All they lack is the food. But they have the weighty menus on their laps – I feel the bottom edge of Trudy's across the small of my back. Now I must listen again to Claude's set piece on menu terms, as if he's the first ever to spot these unimportant absurdities. He lingers on 'pan-fried'. What is *pan* but a deceitful benediction on the vulgar and unhealthy *fried*? Where else might one fry his scallops with chilli and lime juice? In an egg timer? Before moving on, he repeats some of this with a variation of emphasis. Then, his second favourite, an American import, 'steel-cut'. I'm silently mouthing his exposition even before he's begun when a slight tilt in my vertical orientation tells me that my mother is leaning forwards to place a restraining finger on his wrist and say, sweetly, divertingly, 'Choose the wine, darling. Something splendid.'

I like to share a glass with my mother. You may never have experienced, or you will have forgotten, a good burgundy (her favourite) or a good Sancerre (also her favourite) decanted through a healthy placenta. Even before the wine arrives – tonight, a Jean-Max Roger

6

Sancerre – at the sound of a drawn cork, I feel it on my face like the caress of a summer breeze. I know that alcohol will lower my intelligence. It lowers everybody's intelligence. But oh, a joyous, blushful Pinot Noir, or a gooseberried Sauvignon, sets me turning and tumbling across my secret sea, reeling off the walls of my castle, the bouncy castle that is my home. Or so it did when I had more space. Now I take my pleasures sedately, and by the second glass my speculations bloom with that licence whose name is poetry. My thoughts unspool in well-sprung pentameters, end-stopped and run-on lines in pleasing variation. But she never takes a third, and it wounds me.

'I have to think of baby,' I hear her say as she covers her glass with a priggish hand. That's when I have it in mind to reach for my oily cord, as one might a velvet rope in a well-staffed country house, and pull sharply for service. What ho! Another round here for us friends!

But no, she restrains herself for love of me. And I love her – how could I not? The mother I have yet to meet, whom I know only from the inside. Not enough! I long for her external self. Surfaces are everything. I know her hair is 'straw fair', that it tumbles in 'coins of wild curls' to her 'shoulders the white of apple flesh', because my father has read aloud to her his poem about it in my presence. Claude too has referred to her hair in less inventive terms. When she's in the mood, she'll make tight braids to wind around her head, in the style, my father says, of Yulia Tymoshenko. I also know that my mother's eyes are green, that her nose is a 'pearly button', that she wishes she had more of one, that separately both men adore it as it is and have tried to reassure her. She's been told many times that she's beautiful, but she remains sceptical, which confers on her an innocent power over men, so my father told her one afternoon in the library. She replied that if this was true, it was a power she'd never looked for and didn't want. This was an unusual conversation for them and I listened intently. My father, whose name is John, said that if he had such a power over her or women in general, he couldn't imagine giving it up. I guessed, from the sympathetic wave motion which briefly lifted my ear from the wall, that my mother had emphatically shrugged, as if to say, So men are different. Who cares? Besides, she told him out loud, whatever power she was supposed to have was only what men conferred in their fantasies. Then the phone rang, my father walked away to take the call, and this rare and interesting conversation about those that have power was never resumed.

But back to my mother, my untrue Trudy, whose apple-flesh arms and breasts and green regard I long for, whose inexplicable need for Claude pre-dates my first awareness, my primal *is*, and who often speaks to him, and he to her, in pillow whispers, restaurant

8

whispers, kitchen whispers, as if both suspect that wombs have ears.

I used to think that their discretion was no more than ordinary, amorous intimacy. But now I'm certain. They airily bypass their vocal cords because they're planning a dreadful event. Should it go wrong, I've heard them say, their lives will be ruined. They believe that if they're to proceed, they should act quickly, and soon. They tell each other to be calm and patient, remind each other of the cost of their plan's miscarriage, that there are several stages, that each must interlock, that if any single one fails, then all must fail 'like old-fashioned Christmas tree lights' – this impenetrable simile from Claude, who rarely says anything obscure. What they intend sickens and frightens them, and they can never speak of it directly. Instead, wrapped in whispers are ellipses, euphemisms, mumbled aporia followed by throat-clearing and a brisk change of subject.

One hot, restless night last week, when I thought both were long asleep, my mother said suddenly into the darkness, two hours before dawn by the clock downstairs in my father's study, 'We can't do it.'

And straight away Claude said flatly, 'We can.' And then, after a moment's reflection, 'We *can*.'

Now, to my father, John Cairncross, a big man, my genome's other half, whose helical twists of fate concern me greatly. It's in me alone that my parents forever mingle, sweetly, sourly, along separate sugar-phosphate backbones, the recipe for my essential self. I also blend John and Trudy in my daydreams – like every child of estranged parents, I long to remarry them, this base pair, and so unite my circumstances to my genome.

My father comes by the house from time to time and I'm overjoyed. Sometimes he brings her smoothies from his favourite place on Judd Street. He has a weakness for these glutinous confections that are supposed to extend his life. I don't know why he visits us, for he always leaves in mists of sadness. Various of my conjectures have proved wrong in the past, but I've listened carefully and for now I'm assuming the following: that he knows nothing of Claude, remains moonishly in love with my mother, hopes to be back with her one day soon, still believes in the story she has given him that the separation is to give them each 'time and space to grow' and renew their bonds. That he is a poet without recognition and yet he persists. That he owns and runs an impoverished publishing house and has seen into print the first collections of successful poets, household names, and even one Nobel laureate. When their reputations swell, they move away like grown children to larger houses. That he accepts the disloyalty of poets as a fact of life and, like a saint, delights in the plaudits that vindicate the Cairncross Press. That he's saddened rather than embittered by his own failure in verse. He once read aloud to Trudy and me a dismissive review of his poetry. It said that his work was outdated, stiffly formal, too 'beautiful'. But he lives by poetry, still recites it to my mother, teaches it, reviews it, conspires in the advancement of younger poets, sits on prize committees, promotes poetry in schools, writes essays on poetry for small magazines, has talked about it on the radio. Trudy and I heard him once in the small hours. He has less money than Trudy and far less than Claude. He knows by heart a thousand poems.

This is my collection of facts and postulates. Hunched over them like a patient philatelist, I've added some recent items to my set. He suffers from a skin complaint, psoriasis, which has rendered his hands scaly, hard and red. Trudy hates the look and feel of them and tells him he should wear gloves. He refuses. He has a six-month lease on three mean rooms in Shoreditch, is in debt, is overweight and should exercise more. Just yesterday I acquired – still with the stamps – a Penny Black: the house my mother lives in and I in her, the house where

Claude visits nightly, is a Georgian pile on boastful Hamilton Terrace and was my father's childhood home. In his late twenties, just as he was growing his first beard, and not long after he married my mother, he inherited the family mansion. His dear mother was long dead. All the sources agree, the house is filthy. Only clichés serve it well: peeling, crumbling, dilapidated. Frost has sometimes glazed and stiffened the curtains in winter; in heavy rains the drains, like dependable banks, return their deposit with interest; in summer, like bad banks, they stink. But look, here in my tweezers is the rarest piece of all, the British Guiana: even in such a rotten state, these six thousand aching square feet will buy you seven million pounds.

Most men, most people, would never permit a spouse to eject them from under their childhood eaves. John Cairncross is different. Here are my reasonable inferences. Born under an obliging star, eager to please, too kind, too earnest, he has nothing of the ambitious poet's quiet greed. He really believes that to write a poem in praise of my mother (her eyes, her hair, her lips) and come by to read it aloud will soften her, make him welcome in his own house. But she knows that her eyes are nothing 'like the Galway turf', by which he intended 'very green', and since she has no Irish blood, the line is anaemic. Whenever she and I listen, I sense in her slowing heart a retinal crust of boredom that blinds her to the pathos of the scene – a large, large-hearted man pleading his cause without hope, in the unmodish form of a sonnet.

A thousand may be hyperbole. Many of the poems my father knows are long, like those famed creations of bank employees *The Cremation of Sam McGee* and *The Waste Land*. Trudy continues to tolerate the occasional recitation. For her, a monologue is better than an exchange, preferable to another turn round the unweeded garden of their marriage. Perhaps she indulges him out of guilt, what little remains. My father speaking poetry to her was once, apparently, a ritual of their love. Strange, that she can't bear to tell him what he must suspect, what she's bound to reveal. That she no longer loves him. That she has a lover.

On the radio today, a woman recounted hitting a dog, a golden retriever, with her car on a lonely road at night. She crouched in her headlights by its side, holding the dying creature's paw through its spasms of frightful pain. Large brown forgiving eyes stared into hers all the while. She took in her free hand a rock and dashed it several times against the poor dog's skull. To dispatch John Cairncross would take only one blow, one *coup de vérité*. Instead, as he begins to recite, Trudy will assume her bland, listening look. I, however, attend closely.

We generally go to his poetry library on the first floor. A mantelpiece clock with rackety balance wheel makes the only sound as he takes his usual chair. Here, in the presence of a poet, I permit my conjectures to flourish. If my father looks towards the ceiling to compose his thoughts, he'll see deterioration in the Adam-style designs. Damage has spread plaster dust like icing sugar across the spines of famous books. My mother wipes her chair with her hand before she sits. Without flourish, my father draws breath and begins. He recites fluently, with feeling. Most of the modern poems leave me cold. Too much about the self, too glassily cool with regard to others, too many gripes in too short a line. But as warm as the embrace of brothers are John Keats and Wilfred Owen. I feel their breath upon my lips. Their kiss. Who would not wish to have written *Candied apple, quince, and plum and gourd*, or *The pallor of girls' brows shall be their pall*?

I picture her from across the library through his adoring eyes. She sits within a big leather armchair that dates from Freud's Vienna. Her lithe bare legs are partly, prettily tucked beneath her. One elbow is bent against the arm rest to support her drooping head, the fingers of her free hand drum lightly on her ankle. The late afternoon is hot, the windows are open, the traffic of St John's Wood pleasantly hums. Her expression is pensive, her lower lip looks heavy. She moistens it with a spotless tongue. A few blonde ringlets lie damply on her neck. Her cotton dress, loosely cut to contain me, is pale green, paler than her eyes. The steady work of pregnancy goes on and she is weary, agreeably so. John Cairncross sees the summer's flush on her cheeks, the lovely line of neck and shoulder and swollen breasts, the hopeful knoll that is me, the sunless pallor of her calves, the unwrinkled sole of one exposed foot, its line of diminishing, innocent toes like children in a family photo. Everything about her, he thinks, brought to perfection by her condition.

He can't see that she's waiting for him to leave. That it's perverse of her to insist on him living elsewhere, in this, our third trimester. Can he really be so complicit in his annihilation? Such a big fellow, six foot three I've heard, a giant with thick black hair on mighty arms, a giant fool to believe it's wise to grant his wife the 'space' she says she needs. Space! She should come in here, where lately I can barely crook a finger. In my mother's usage, space, her need for it, is a misshapen metaphor, if not a synonym. For being selfish, devious, cruel. But wait, I love her, she's my divinity and I need her. I take it back! I spoke in anguish. I'm as deluded as my father. And it's true. Her beauty and remoteness and resolve are one.

Above her, as I see it, the library's decomposing ceiling releases a sudden cloud of spinning particles that glimmer as they drift across a bar of sunlight. And how she glimmers against the cracked brown leather of the chair where Hitler or Trotsky or Stalin might have sprawled in their Viennese days, when they were but embryos of their future selves. I concede. I'm hers. If she commanded it, I too would go to Shoreditch, and nurse myself in exile. No need for an umbilical cord. My father and I are joined in hopeless love.

Against all the signs – her terse responses, her yawns, her general inattention – he lingers into the early evening, in hopes, perhaps, of dinner. But my mother is waiting for Claude. At last she drives her husband away by declaring her need to rest. She'll see him to the door. Who could ignore the sorrow in his voice as he makes his tentative goodbyes. It pains me to think he would endure any humiliation in order to spend some minutes longer in her presence. Nothing, save his nature, prevents him doing what others might do – precede her to the master bedroom, to the room where he and I were conceived, sprawl on the bed or in the tub among bold clouds of steam, then invite his friends round, pour wine, be master of his house. Instead, he hopes to succeed by kindness and self-effacing sensitivity to her needs. I hope to be wrong, but I think he'll doubly fail, for she'll go on despising him for being weak, and he'll suffer even more than he should. His visits don't end, they fade. He leaves behind in the library a field of resonating sadness, an imagined shape, a disappointed hologram still in possession of his chair.

Now we're approaching the front door as she sees him off the premises. These various depredations have been much discussed. I know that one hinge of this door has parted with the woodwork. Dry rot has turned the architrave to compacted dust. Some floor tiles have gone, others are cracked – Georgian, in a once colourful diamond pattern, impossible to replace. Concealing those absences and cracks, plastic bags of empty bottles and rotting food. Spilling underfoot, these are the very emblems of household squalor: the detritus of ashtrays, paper plates with loathsome wounds of ketchup, teetering teabags like tiny sacks of grain that mice or elves might hoard. The cleaning lady left in sadness long before my time. Trudy knows it's not a gravid woman's lot, to heave garbage to the high-lidded wheelie bins. She could easily ask my father to clean the hall, but she doesn't. Household duties might confer household rights. And she may be at work on a clever story of his desertion. Claude remains in this respect a visitor, an outsider, but I've heard him say that to tidy one corner of the house would be to foreground the chaos in the rest. Despite the heatwave I'm well protected against the stench. My mother complains about it most days, but languidly. It's only one aspect of domestic decay.

She may think that a blob of curd on his shoe, or the sight of a cobalt-furred orange by the skirting will shorten my father's goodbyes. She's wrong. The door is open, he straddles the threshold and she and I are just inside the hall. Claude is due in fifteen minutes. He sometimes comes early. So Trudy is agitated but determined to appear sleepy. She's standing on eggshells. A square of greasy paper that once wrapped a slab of unsalted butter is caught under her sandal and has oiled her toes. This she will soon relate to Claude in humorous terms.

My father says, 'Look, we really must talk.'

'Yes, but not now.'

'We keep putting it off.'

'I can't begin to tell you how tired I am. You've no idea what it's like. I've simply got to lie down.'

'Of course. That's why I'm thinking of moving back in, so I can—'

'Please John, not now. We've been through this. I need more time. Try to be considerate. I'm bearing your child, remember? This isn't the time to be thinking of yourself.'

'I don't like you being alone here when I could—'

'John!'

I hear his sigh as he embraces her as closely as she'll permit. Next, I feel her arm go out to take his wrist, carefully avoiding, I should think, his afflicted hands, turn him and gently propel him towards the street.

'Darling, please, just *go* . . .'

Later, while my mother reclines, angry and exhausted, I recede into primal speculation. What kind of being is this? Is big John Cairncross our envoy to the future, the form of a man to end wars, rapine and enslavement and stand equal and caring with the women of the world? Or will he be trampled into oblivion by brutes? We shall find out.

THREE

WHO IS THIS CLAUDE, this fraud who's wormed in between my family and my hopes? I heard it once and took note: *the dull-brained yokel*. My full prospects are dimmed. His existence denies my rightful claims to a happy life in the care of both parents. Unless I devise a plan. He has entranced my mother and banished my father. His interests can't be mine. He'll crush me. Unless, unless, unless – a wisp of a word, ghostly token of altered fate, bleating little iamb of hope, it drifts across my thoughts like a floater in the vitreous humour of an eye. Mere hope.

And Claude, like a floater, is barely real. Not even a colourful chancer, no hint of the smiling rogue. Instead, dull to the point of brilliance, vapid beyond invention, his banality as finely wrought as the arabesques of the Blue Mosque. Here is a man who whistles continually, not songs but TV jingles, ringtones, who brightens a morning with Nokia's mockery of Tárrega. Whose repeated remarks are a witless, thrustless dribble, whose impoverished sentences die like motherless chicks, cheaply fading. Who washes his private parts at the basin where my mother washes her face. Who knows only clothes and cars. And has told us a hundred times that he would never buy or even drive such, or such, or a hybrid or a . . . or . . . That he only buys his suits in this, no, that Mayfair street, his shirts in some other, and socks from, he can't recall . . . If only . . . but. No one else ends a sentence on a 'but'.

That stale, uncertain voice. My entire life I've endured the twin torments of his whistling and his speaking. I've been spared the sight of him, but that will soon change. In the dim-lit gore of the delivery room (Trudy has decided that he, not my father, will be there), when I emerge to greet him at last, my questions will remain, whatever form he takes: what is my mother *doing*? What can she want? Has she conjured Claude to illustrate the enigma of the erotic?

Not everyone knows what it is to have your father's rival's penis inches from your nose. By this late stage they should be refraining on my behalf. Courtesy, if not clinical judgement, demands it. I close my eyes, I grit my gums, I brace myself against the uterine walls. This turbulence would shake the wings off a Boeing. My mother goads her lover, whips him on with her fairground shrieks. Wall of Death! On each occasion, on every piston stroke, I dread that he'll break through and shaft my soft-boned skull and seed my thoughts with his essence, with the teeming cream of his banality. Then, brain-damaged, I'll think and speak like him. I'll be the son of Claude.

But rather trap me inside a wingless Boeing's mid-Atlantic plunge than book me one more night of his foreplay. Here I am, in the front stalls, awkwardly seated upside down. This is a minimal production, bleakly modern, a two-hander. The lights are full on, and here comes Claude. It's himself, not my mother, he intends to undress. He neatly folds his clothes across a chair. His nakedness is as unstartling as an accountant's suit. He wanders about the bedroom, upstage, down-stage, bare-skinned through the soft drizzle of his soliloquy. His aunt's pink birthday soap that he must return to Curzon Street, a mostly forgotten dream he had, the price of diesel, it feels like Tuesday. But it's not. Each brave new topic rises groaning to its feet, totters, then falls to the next. And my mother? On the bed, between the sheets, partly dressed, wholly attentive, with ready hums and sympathetic nods. Known only to me, under the bedclothes, a forefinger curls over her modest clitoral snood and rests a sweet half-inch inside her. This finger she gently rocks as she concedes everything and offers up her soul. I assume it's delicious to do so. Yes, she murmurs through her sighs, she too had her doubts about the soap, yes, her dreams are also lost to her too soon, she too thinks it's Tuesday. Nothing about diesel – a small mercy.

His knees depress the unfaithful mattress that lately held my father. With able thumbs she hooks her panties clear. Enter Claude. Sometimes he'll call her his mouse, which seems to please her, but no kisses, nothing touched or fondled, or murmured or promised, no licks of kindness, no playful daydreams. Only the accelerating creak of the bed, until at last my mother arrives to take her place on the Wall of Death and begins to scream. You might know this old-fashioned attraction of the funfair. As it turns and accelerates, centrifugal force pins you against the wall while the floor beneath you drops giddily away. Trudy spins faster, her face is a blur of strawberries and cream, and a green smear of angelica where her eyes once were. She screams louder, then, after her final rising-falling shout-and-shudder, I hear his abrupt, strangled grunt. The briefest pause. Exit Claude. The mattress dips again and his voice resumes, now from the bathroom – a reprise of Curzon Street or the day of the week, and some cheerful assays on the Nokia theme. One act, three minutes at most, no repeats. Often she joins him in the bathroom and, without touching, they expunge each other from their bodies with absolving hot water. Nothing tender, no fond dozing in a lovers' tangled clasp. During this brisk ablution, minds swabbed clean by orgasm, they often turn to plotting, but in the room's tiled echo, against running taps, their words are lost to me.

Which is why I know so little of their plan. Only that it excites them, lowers their voices, even when they think they're alone. Nor do I know Claude's surname. By profession a property developer, though not as successful as most. The brief and profitable ownership of a tower block in Cardiff was one peak of his achievement. Wealthy? Inherited a seven-figure sum, now down, it seems, to his last quarter-million. He leaves our house around ten, returns after six. Here are two opposing propositions: the first, a firmer personality lurks inside a shell of blandness. To be this insipid is hardly plausible. Someone clever and dark and calculating is hiding in there. As a man he's a piece of work, a self-constructed device, a tool for hard deception, scheming against Trudy even as he schemes beside her. The second, he's as he appears, the cockle has no morsel, he's as honest a schemer as she, only dimmer. For her part, she'd rather not doubt a man who hurls her over the gates of paradise in under three minutes. Whereas I keep an open mind.

My hope of discovering more is to wait up all night to catch them in one more disinhibited aubade. Claude's untypical 'we can' first caused me to doubt his dullness. Five days have since passed – and nothing. I kick my mother awake but she won't disturb her lover. Instead she clamps a podcast lecture to her ears and submits to the wonders of the Internet. She listens at random. I've heard it all. Maggot farming in Utah. Hiking across The Burren. Hitler's last-chance offensive in the Ardennes.

Sexual etiquette among the Yanomami. How Poggio Bracciolini rescued Lucretius from oblivion. The physics of tennis.

I stay awake, I listen, I learn. Early this morning, less than an hour before dawn, there was heavier matter than usual. Through my mother's bones I encountered a bad dream in the guise of a formal lecture. The state of the world. An expert in international relations, a reasonable woman with a rich deep voice, advised me that the world was not well. She considered two common states of mind: self-pity and aggression. Each one a poor choice for individuals. In combination, for groups or nations, a noxious brew that lately intoxicated the Russians in Ukraine, as it once had their friends, the Serbs in their part of the world. We were belittled, now we will prove ourselves. Now that the Russian state was the political arm of organised crime, another war in Europe no longer inconceivable. Dust down the tank divisions for Lithuania's southern border, for the north German plain. The same potion inflames the barbaric fringes of Islam. The cup is drained, the same cry goes up: we've been humiliated, we'll be avenged.

The lecturer took a dim view of our species, of which psychopaths are a constant fraction, a human constant. Armed struggle, just or not, attracts them. They help to tip local struggles into bigger conflicts. Europe, according to her, in existential crisis, fractious and weak as varieties of self-loving nationalism sip that same tasty brew. Confusion about values, the bacillus of anti-Semitism incubating, immigrant populations languishing, angry and bored. Elsewhere, everywhere, novel inequalities of wealth, the super rich a master race apart. Ingenuity deployed by states for new forms of brilliant weaponry, by global corporations to dodge taxes, by righteous banks to stuff themselves with Christmas millions. China, too big to need friends or counsel, cynically probing its neighbours' shores, building islands of tropical sand, planning for the war it knows must come. Muslim-majority countries plagued by religious puritanism, by sexual sickness, by smothered invention. The Middle East, fast-breeder for a possible world war. And foe-of-convenience, the United States, barely the hope of the world, guilty of torture, helpless before its sacred text conceived in an age of powdered wigs, a constitution as unchallengeable as the Koran. Its nervous population obese, fearful, tormented by inarticulate anger, contemp-tuous of governance, murdering sleep with every new handgun. Africa yet to learn democracy's party trick – the peaceful transfer of power. Its children dying, thousands by the week, for want of easy things – clean water, mosquito nets, cheap drugs. Uniting and levelling all humanity, the dull old facts of altered climate, vanishing forests, creatures and polar ice. Profitable and poisonous agriculture obliterating biological beauty.

Oceans turning to weak acid. Well above the horizon, approaching fast, the urinous tsunami of the burgeoning old, cancerous and demented, demanding care. And soon, with demographic transition, the reverse, populations in catastrophic decline. Free speech no longer free, liberal democracy no longer the obvious port of destiny, robots stealing jobs, liberty in close combat with security, socialism in disgrace, capitalism corrupt, destructive and in disgrace, no alternatives in sight.

In conclusion, she said, these disasters are the work of our twin natures. Clever and infantile. We've built a world too complicated and dangerous for our quarrelsome natures to manage. In such hopelessness, the general vote will be for the supernatural. It's dusk in the second Age of Reason. We were wonderful, but now we are doomed. Twenty minutes. Click.

Anxiously, I finger my cord. It serves for worry beads. Wait, I thought. While it lies ahead of me, what's wrong with infantile? I've heard enough of such talks to have learned to summon the counterarguments. Pessimism is too easy, even delicious, the badge and plume of intellectuals everywhere. It absolves the thinking classes of solutions. We excite ourselves with dark thoughts in plays, poems, novels, movies. And now in commentaries. Why trust this account when humanity has never been so rich, so healthy, so long-lived? When fewer die in wars and childbirth than ever before – and more knowledge, more truth by way of science, was never so available to us all? When tender sympathies – for children, animals, alien religions, unknown, distant foreigners – swell daily? When hundreds of millions have been raised from wretched subsistence? When, in the West, even the middling poor recline in armchairs, charmed by music as they steer themselves down smooth highways at four times the speed of a galloping horse? When smallpox, polio, cholera, measles, high infant mortality, illiteracy, public executions and routine state torture have been banished from so many countries? Not so long ago, all these curses were everywhere. When solar panels and wind farms and nuclear energy and inventions not yet known will deliver us from the sewage of carbon dioxide, and GM crops will save us from the ravages of chemical farming and the poorest from starvation? When the worldwide migration to the cities will return vast tracts of land to wilderness, will lower birth rates, and rescue women from ignorant village patriarchs? What of the commonplace miracles that would make a manual labourer the envy of Caesar Augustus: pain-free dentistry, electric light, instant contact with people we love, with the best music the world has known, with the cuisine of a dozen cultures? We're bloated with privileges and delights, as well as complaints, and the rest who are not will be soon. As for the Russians, the same was said of Catholic Spain. We expected their armies on our beaches.

Like most things, it didn't happen. The matter was settled by some fireships and a useful storm that drove their fleet round the top of Scotland. We'll always be troubled by how things are – that's how it stands with the difficult gift of consciousness.

Just one hymn to the golden world I'm about to possess. In my confinement I've become a connoisseur of collective dreams. Who knows what's true? I can hardly collect the evidence for myself. Every proposition is matched or cancelled by another. Like everyone else, I'll take what I want, whatever suits me.

But these reflections have been distracting me and I've missed the first words of the exchange I've stayed awake to hear. The aubade. The alarm was minutes from sounding, Claude murmured something, my mother replied, then he spoke again. I come round, I press my ear to the wall. I feel a disturbance in the mattress. The night has been warm. Claude must be sitting up, pulling off the T-shirt he wears to bed. I hear him say he's meeting his brother this afternoon. He's mentioned this brother before. I should have paid more attention. But the context has generally bored me – money, accounts, taxes, debts.

Claude says, 'All his hopes are on this poet he's signing up.'

Poet? Very few people in the world sign up a poet. I only know of one. His *brother*?

My mother says, 'Ah yes, this woman. Forgotten her name. Writes about owls.'

'Owls! A hot topic is owls! But I should see him tonight.'

She says slowly, 'I don't think you should. Not now.'

'Or he'll come round here again. I don't want him bothering you. But.'

My mother says, 'Nor do I. But this has to be done my way. Slowly.'

There's a silence. Claude takes his phone from the bedside table and pre-emptively turns off the alarm.

Finally he says, 'If I lend my brother money it'll be good cover.'

'But not too much. We won't exactly be getting it back.'

They laugh. Then Claude and his whistling make for the bathroom, my mother turns on her side and goes back to sleep, and I'm left in the dark to confront the outrageous fact and consider my stupidity.

FOUR

When I hear the friendly drone of passing cars and a slight breeze stirs what I believe are horse chestnut leaves, when a portable radio below me tinnily rasps and a penumbral coral glow, a prolonged tropical dusk, dully illuminates my inland sea and its trillion drifting fragments, then I know that my mother is sunbathing on the balcony outside my father's library. I know too that the ornate cast-iron railing of oak leaf and acorn design is held together by historical layers of black paint and should not be leaned on. The cantilevered shelf of crumbling concrete where my mother sits has been declared unsafe, even by builders with no interest in the repairs. The balcony's narrow width permits a deckchair to be placed obliquely, almost parallel to the house. Trudy is barefoot, in bikini top, and brief denim shorts that barely allow for me. Pink-framed, heart-shaped sunglasses and a straw hat top this confection. I know this because my uncle – my *uncle*! – asked her on the phone to tell him what she was wearing. Flirtatiously, she obliged.

A few minutes ago the radio told us it was four o'clock. We're sharing a glass, perhaps a bottle, of Marlborough Sauvignon Blanc. Not my first choice, and for the same grape and a less grassy taste, I would have gone for a Sancerre, preferably from Chavignol. A degree of flinty mineral definition would have mitigated the blunt assault of direct sunlight and oven blast of heat reflected off the cracked facade of our house.

But we're in New Zealand, it's in us, and I'm happier than I've been for two days. Trudy cools our wine with plastic cubes of frozen ethanol. I've nothing against that. I'm offered my first intimation of colour and shape, for my mother's midriff is angled towards the sun, so I can make out, as in the reddish blur of a photographic dark-room, my hands in front of my face and the cord amply tangled around belly and knees. I see that my fingernails need clipping, though I'm not expected for two weeks. I'd like to think that her purpose out here is to generate vitamin D for my bone growth, that she has turned down the radio the better to contemplate my existence, that the hand caressing the place where she believes my head to be is an expression of tenderness. But she may be working on her tan and too hot to listen to the radio drama about the Mughal emperor Aurangzeb, and is merely soothing with her fingertips the bloated discomfort of late pregnancy. In short, I am uncertain of her love.

Wine after three glasses solves nothing and the pain of recent discovery remains. Still, I'm feeling a friendly touch of disassociation: I'm already some useful steps removed and see myself revealed some fifteen feet below me, like a fallen climber spreadeagled and supine on a rock. I can begin to comprehend my situation, I can think as well as feel. An unassuming New World white can do this much. So. My mother has preferred my father's brother, cheated her husband, ruined her son. My uncle has stolen his brother's wife, deceived his nephew's father, grossly insulted his sister-in-law's son. My father by nature is defenceless, as I am by circumstance. My uncle – a quarter of my genome, of my father's a half, but no more like my father than I to Virgil or Montaigne. What despicable part of myself is Claude and how will I know? I could be my own brother and deceive myself as he deceived his. When I'm born and allowed at last to be alone, there's a quarter I'll want to take a kitchen knife to. But the one who holds the knife will also be my uncle, quartering in my genome. Then we'll see how the knife won't move. And this perception too is somewhat his. And this.

My affair with Trudy isn't going well. I thought I could take her love for granted. But I've heard biologists debating at dawn. Pregnant mothers must fight the tenants of their wombs. Nature, a mother herself, ordains a struggle for resources that may be needed to nurture my future sibling rivals. My health derives from Trudy, but she must preserve herself against me. So why would she worry about my *feelings*? If it's in her interests and those of some unconceived squit that I should be under-nourished, why trouble herself if a tryst with my uncle upsets me? The biologists also suggest that my father's wisest move is to trick another man into raising his child while he – my father! – distributes his likeness among other women. So bleak, so loveless. We're alone then, all of us, even me, each treading a deserted highway, toting in a bundle on a shouldered stick the schemes, the flow charts, for unconscious advancement.

Too much to bear, too grim to be true. Why would the world configure itself so harshly? Among much else, people are sociable and kind. Ripeness isn't everything. My mother is more than my landlord. My father longs not for the widest dissemination of his selfhood, but for his wife and, surely, his only son. I don't believe the sages of the life sciences. He must love me, wants to move back in, will care for me – given the chance. And she's never caused me to miss a meal, and until this afternoon has decently refused a third glass on my account. It's not her love that's failing. It's mine. It's my resentment that falls between us. I refuse to say I hate her. But to abandon a poet, any poet, for Claude!

That's hard, and what's also hard is that the poet is so soft. John Cairncross, ousted from his family home, his grandfather's purchase, for a philosophy of 'personal growth' – a phrase as paradoxical as 'easy listening'. To be apart so they can be together, turn their backs so they might embrace, stop loving so they can fall in love. He bought it. What a sap! Between his weakness and her deceit was the fetid crack that spontaneously generated a maggot-uncle. And I squat here sealed in my private life, in a lingering, sultry dusk, impatiently dreaming.

What I could do if instead I was at my peak. Let's say twenty-eight years from now. Jeans faded and tight, abs tight and ridged, moving sleekly like a panther, temporarily immortal. Fetching my ancient father in a taxi from Shoreditch to install him, deaf to Trudy's matronly protests, in his library, in his bed. Catching old Uncle Maggot by the neck to toss him into the leafy gutter of Hamilton Terrace. Hushing my mother with a careless kiss to her nape.

But here's life's most limiting truth – it's always now, always here, never then and there. And now we are frying in a London heatwave, here on an unsound balcony. I listen to her refill the glass, the plop of plastic cubes, her soft sigh, more anxious than content. A fourth glass then. She must think I'm old enough to take it. And I am. We're getting drunk because even now her lover is conferring with his brother in the windowless office of the Cairncross Press.

To divert myself I send my thoughts ahead to spy on them. Purely an exercise of the imagination. Nothing here is real.

The soft loan is laid out on the crowded desk.

'John, she truly loves you but she's asked me as trusted family member to ask you to stay away for just a little while. Best hope for your marriage. Erm. It'll come out right in the end. I should've guessed your rent was in arrears. But. Please say yes, take the cash, let her have her space.'

It sits between them on the desk, five thousand pounds in filthy fifties, five odorous heaps of red script. To each side are poetry books and typescripts loosely piled, sharpened pencils, and two glass ashtrays, well filled, a bottle of Scotch, a gentle Tomintoul with an inch remaining, a crystal tumbler, a dead fly on its back inside, several aspirins lying on an unused tissue. Squalid marks of honest toil.

My guess is this. My father has never understood his younger brother. Never thought it worth the sweat. And John doesn't like a confrontation. His gaze won't meet the money on the desk. It wouldn't occur to him to explain that returning home to be with wife and child is all he wants.

Instead he says, 'This came in yesterday. Would you like to hear a poem about an owl?'

Just the kind of irrelevant whimsy that Claude hated as a child. He shakes his head, *no please spare me*, but it's too late.

My father has a single sheet of typescript in his scaly hand.

'Blood-wise fatal bellman,' he starts. He likes a trochaic trimeter.

'You don't want it then,' his brother sulkily interrupts. 'Fine by me.' And with banker's wormy fingers collates the piles, soft-drops the edges against the surface of the desk, from nowhere takes a rubber band and in two seconds he's returned the cash to an inside pocket of his silver-buttoned blazer, and stands, looking hot and sick.

My father, unrushed, reads the second line. 'We quaintly thrill to a shrieking cruelty.' Then he stops and mildly says, 'Do you have to go?'

No close observer could decode the sibling shorthand, the time-bound sadness of this exchange. The rates, the rules, were set too long ago to be revised. Claude's relative wealth must go unrecognised. He remains the younger brother, inadequate, strangled, furious. My father is puzzled by his closest living relative, but only faintly. He won't move off his ground and from it sounds mocking. But he isn't. It's worse than mockery: he doesn't care, and hardly knows he doesn't care. About rent, or money or Claude's offer. But because he's a considerate man he stands politely to see his visitor out, and when that's done and he's sitting at his desk again, the cash that was there is forgotten, and so is Claude. The pencil's back in my father's hand, a cigarette's in the other. He'll go on with the only work that matters, proofing poems for the printers, and won't look up until it's six and time for a whisky and water. First he'll tip the fly from the tumbler.

As though from a long journey, I return to the womb. Nothing has changed on the balcony, except I find myself a tad drunker. As if to welcome me back, Trudy drains the bottle into her glass. The cubes have lost their cool, the wine is almost warm, but she's right, better to finish it now. It won't keep. The breeze still stirs the chestnut trees, the afternoon traffic is picking up. As the sun descends, it feels warmer. But I don't mind the heat. As the last of the Sauvignon Blanc arrives I set myself to reconsider. I've been away, I escaped over the wire without ladder or rope, free as a bird, leaving behind my now and my here. My limiting truth was untrue: I can be gone any time I like, throw Claude out the house, visit my father in his office, be a loving, invisible snooper. Are movies as good as this? I'll find out. One could make a living devising such excursions. But the actual, the circumscribed real, is absorbing too and I'm impatient for Claude to return and tell us what really happened. My version is certain to be wrong.

My mother is also anxious to know. If she wasn't drinking for two, if I wasn't sharing the load, she'd be on the floor. After twenty minutes we go indoors and make our way across the library, then upstairs towards the bedroom. One should be careful, going barefoot through this house. My mother yelps as something crunches underfoot, we pitch and yaw as she lunges at the banister. Then we're steady while she pauses to inspect her sole. Her curse is muttered calmly, so there must be blood, but not too much. She hobbles through the bedroom, leaving a trail perhaps on what I know to be a filthy off-white carpet strewn with discarded clothes and shoes and suitcases half unpacked from journeys that pre-date my time.

We reach the echoey bathroom, a large and filthy shambles, from what I've heard. She pulls open a drawer, impatiently stirs its rattling, rustling contents, tries another, and in the third locates the plaster for her cut. She sits on the edge of the bath and rests her poor foot across her knee. Little grunts and gasps of exasperation suggest her cut's in a place that's hard to reach. If only I could kneel before her and help. Even though she's young and slim, it's not easy leaning forwards with my impeding bulk. Better then, she decides, more stable, to clear a space and sit down on the hard tiled floor. But that's not easy either. It's all my fault.

This is where we are and what we're doing when we hear Claude's voice, a shout from down the stairs.

'Trudy! Oh my God. Trudy!'

The thump of rapid footsteps, and he shouts her name again. Then, his heavy breathing in the bathroom.

'I cut my foot on a stupid piece of glass.'

'There's blood all through the bedroom. I thought . . .' He doesn't tell us that he hoped for my demise. Instead he says, 'Let me do it. Shouldn't we clean it first?'

'Stick it on.'

'Hold still.' Now his turn to grunt and gasp. And then, 'Have you been drinking?'

'Fuck off. Stick it on.'

At last it's done and he helps her to her feet. Together we sway.

'Christ! How much did you have?'

'Just a glass.'

She rests again on the bathtub's rim.

He steps away, into the bedroom, and returns a minute later. 'We'll never get that blood off the carpet.'

'Try rubbing it with something.'

'I'm telling you, it won't come out. Look. Here's a spot. Try it yourself.'

I've rarely heard Claude so forthright. Not since 'We can.'

My mother too hears the difference and says, 'What happened?'

Now there's a whine of complaint in his voice.

'He took the money, didn't thank me for it. And get this. He's given his notice on the Shoreditch place. He's moving back in here. He says you need him, however much you say you don't.'

The bathroom echoes die away. But for their breathing, there's silence while they consider. My guess is they're looking at each other, into each other, a long, eloquent stare.

'There it is,' he says at last, in his familiar, empty way. He waits, then adds, 'So?'

At this my mother's heart begins a steady acceleration. Not just faster, but louder, like the hollow knocking sound of faulty plumbing. Something is also happening in her gut. Her bowels are loosening, with a squeaky stretching sound, and higher up, somewhere above my feet, juices race down winding tubes to unknown destinations. Her diaphragm heaves. I'm pressing my ear more tightly to the wall. Against this crescendo, it would be too easy to miss a vital fact.

The body cannot lie, but the mind is another country, for when my mother speaks at last, her tone is smooth, nicely in control. 'I agree.'

Claude comes closer, speaks softly, almost at a whisper. 'But. What do you think?'

They kiss and she starts to tremble. I feel his arms move round her waist. They kiss again with soundless tongues.

She says, 'Scary.'

And responding to a private joke he replies, 'Hairy.'

But they fail to laugh. I feel Claude push his groin into hers. That they should be aroused at such a time!

How little I know. She finds his zip, tugs downwards, caresses, while his index finger curls under her cut-offs. I feel its recurrent pressure on my forehead. Might we go upstairs? But no, thank God, he pursues his question.

'Decide.'

'I'm frightened.'

'But remember. Six months ahead. In my house, seven million in the bank. And we've placed the baby somewhere. But. What's it to. Erm. Be?'

His own practical question calms him, allows him to withdraw his finger. But her pulse, which had begun to settle, leaps at his question. Not sex but danger. Her blood beats through me in thuds like distant artillery fire and I can feel her struggling with a choice. I'm an organ in her body, not separate from her thoughts. I'm party to what she's about to do. When it comes at last, her decision, her whispered command, her single treacherous utterance, appears to issue from my own untried mouth. As they kiss again she says it into her lover's mouth. Baby's first word.

'Poison.'

FIVE

How solipsism becomes the unborn. While bare-foot Trudy sleeps off our five glasses on the sitting-room couch and our dirty house rolls eastwards into thick night, I dwell as much on my uncle's *placed* as my mother's *poison*. Like a DJ hunched over his turntable, I scratchily sample the line. *And . . . we've placed the baby somewhere*. With repetition, the words are rubbed clean as truth and my intended future shines clear. *Placed* is but the lying cognate of *dumped*. As *the baby* is of *me*. *Somewhere* is a liar too. Ruthless mother! This will be an undoing, my fall, for only in fairy tales are unwanted babies orphaned upwards. The Duchess of Cambridge will not be taking me on. My solo flight of self-pity settles me somewhere on the thirteenth floor of the brutal tower block my mother says she sometimes gazes on sadly from an upper bedroom window. She gazes and thinks, So close, yet remote as the Vale of Swat. Fancy living there.

Quite so. Raised bookless on computer toys, sugar, fat and smacks to the head. Swat indeed. No bedtime stories to nourish my toddler brain's plasticity. The curiosity-free mindscape of the modern English peasantry. What then of maggot farming in Utah? Poor me, poor buzz-cut, barrel-chested three-year-old boy in camou-flage trousers, lost in a haze of TV noise and secondary smoke. His adoptive mother's tattooed and swollen ankles totter past, followed by her labile boyfriend's pungent dog. Beloved father, rescue me from this Vale of Despond. Take me down with you. Let me be poisoned at your side rather than *placed somewhere*.

Typical third-term self-indulgence. All I know of the English poor has come to me by way of TV and reviews of novelistic mockery. I know nothing. But my reasonable suspicion is that poverty is deprivation on all levels. No harpsichord lessons on the thirteenth floor. If hypocrisy's the only price, I'll buy the bourgeois life and consider it cheap. And more, I'll hoard grain, be rich, have a coat of arms. NON SANZ DROICT, and mine is to a mother's love and is absolute. To her schemes of abandonment I deny consent. I won't be exiled, but she will be. I'll bind her with this slimy rope, press-gang her on my birthday with one groggy, newborn stare, one lonesome seagull wail to harpoon her heart. Then, indentured by strong-armed love to become my constant nurse, her freedom but a retreating homeland shore, Trudy will be mine, not Claude's, as able to dump me as tear her breasts from her ribcage and toss them over-board. I can be ruthless too.

* * *

44

And so I went on, drunkenly, I suppose, expansive and irrelevant, until she woke with several groans and fumbled for her sandals under the couch. Together we descend, limping, to the humid kitchen, where, in the semi-darkness that might almost hide the squalor, she bends to drink at length from the cold-water tap. Still in her beachwear. She turns on the lights. No sign of Claude, no note. We go to the fridge and hopefully she looks in. I see – I imagine I see on an untested retina – her pale, indecisive arm hovering in the cold light. I love her beautiful arm. On a lower shelf something once living, now purulent, appears to stir in its paper bag, drawing from her a reverential gasp, forcing her to close the door. So we cross the room to the dry-goods cupboard and there she finds a bag of salted nuts. Shortly, I hear her dial her lover.

'Are you still at home?'

I can't hear him for her crunching.

'Well,' she says, after listening. 'Bring it here. We need to talk.'

From the gentle way she sets down the phone I assume he's on his way. Bad enough. But I'm having my very first headache, right around the forehead, a gaudy bandanna, a carefree pain dancing to her pulse. If she'd share it with me, she might reach for an analgesic. By rights, the pain is hers. But she's braving the fridge again and has found high in the door, on a Perspex shelf, a nine-inch wedge of historic parmesan as old as evil, as hard as adamantine. If she can break into it with her teeth, we'll suffer together, after the nuts, a second incoming salt tide rolling through the estuary inlets, thickening our blood to brackish ooze. Water, she should drink more water. My hands drift upwards to find my temples. Monstrous injustice, to have such pain before my life's begun.

I've heard it argued that long ago pain begat consciousness. To avoid serious damage a simple creature needs to evolve the whips and goads of a subjective loop, of a felt experience. Not just a red warning light in the head – who's there to see it? – but a sting, an ache, a throb that *hurts*. Adversity forced awareness on us, and it works, it bites us when we go too near the fire, when we love too hard. Those felt sensations are the beginning of the invention of the self. And if that works, why not feeling disgust for shit, fearing the cliff edge and strangers, remembering insults and favours, liking sex and food? God said, Let there be pain. And there was poetry. Eventually.

So what's the use of a headache, a heartache? What am I being warned against, or told what to do? Don't let your incestuous uncle and mother poison your father. Don't waste your precious days idle and inverted. Get born and act!

She sets herself down on a kitchen chair with a

hung-over groan, the elective malady's melody. There are not many options for the evening that follows an afternoon of drinking. Only two in fact: remorse, or more drinking and then remorse. She's chosen the first, but it's early yet. The cheese is on the table, already forgotten. Claude is returning from where my mother will live, a millionairess shot of me. He'll cross London by cab because he's never learned to drive.

I try to see her as she is, as she must be, the gravidly ripe twenty-eight-year-old, youngly slumped (I insist on the adverb) across the table, blonde and braided like a Saxon warrior, beautiful beyond realism's reach, slender but for me, near naked, sunnily pink on the upper arms, finding space on the kitchen table for her elbows among the yolk-glazed plates of a month ago, the toast and sugar crumbs that houseflies daily vomit on, the reeking cartons and coated spoons, the fluids dried to scabs on junk-mail envelopes. I try to see her and love her as I must, then imagine her burdens: the villain she's taken for a lover, the saint she's leaving behind, the deed she's spoken for, the darling child she'll abandon to strangers. Still love her? If not, then you never did. But I did, I did. I do.

She remembers the cheese and reaches for the nearest tool and makes a decent stab. A piece snaps off and it's in her mouth, a dry rock to suck on while she considers her state. Some minutes pass. Not good, I think, her state, though our blood won't thicken after all, because the salt she's eating she'll need for her eyes, her cheeks. It pierces the child, to hear the mother cry. She's confronting the unanswerable world she's made, of all that she's consented to, her new duties, which I need to list again – kill John Cairncross, sell his birthright, share the money, dump the kid. It should be me who weeps. But the unborn are po-faced stoics, submerged Buddhas, expressionless. We accept, as our lesser kith the wailing babies don't, that tears are in the nature of things. *Sunt lacrimae rerum.* Infantile wailing entirely misses the point. Waiting is the thing. And thinking!

She's recovered by the time we hear her lover in the hall, cursing as he disturbs the garbage with the outsized brogues she likes him to wear. (He has his own key. It's my father who has to ring the bell.) Claude descends to the basement kitchen. The rustling sound is a plastic bag containing groceries or tools of death or both.

He notices at once her altered condition and says, 'You've been crying.'

Not solicitude so much as a point of fact, or order. She shrugs and looks away. He takes from his bag a bottle, sets it down heavily where she can see the label.

'A 2010 Cuvée le Charnay Menetou-Salon Jean-Max Roger. Remember? His neighbour, Didier Dagueneau died in a plane crash.'

He speaks of the death of fathers.

'If it's cold and white I'll like it.'

She's forgotten. The restaurant where the waiter was slow to light the candle. She loved it then, and I loved it even more. Now, the withdrawn cork, the chink of glasses – I hope they're clean – and Claude is pouring. I can't say no.

'Cheers!' Her tone has quickly softened.

A top-up, then he says, 'Tell me what it was.'

When she starts to speak her throat constricts. 'I was thinking of our cat. I was fifteen. His name was Hector, a sweet old thing, the family's darling, two years older than me. Black, with white socks and bib. I came home from school one day in a filthy mood. He was on the kitchen table where he wasn't supposed to be. Looking for food. I gave him a whack that knocked him flying. His old bones landed with a crunch. After that he went missing for days. We put posters on trees and lamp posts. Then someone found him lying by a wall on a heap of leaves where he'd crept away to die. Poor, poor Hector, stiff as bone. I never said, I never dared, but I know it was me who killed him.'

Not her wicked undertaking then, not lost innocence, not the child she'll give away. She begins to cry again, harder than before.

'His time was almost up,' Claude says. 'You can't know it was you.'

Sobbing now. 'It was, it was. It was me! Oh God!'

I know, I know. Where did I hear it? – *He kills his*

mother but he can't wear grey trousers. But let's be generous. A young woman, gut and breasts swollen to breaking, God-mandated pain looming, milk and shit to follow and sleepless trek through a new-found land of unenchanting duties, where brutal love will steal her life – and the ghost of an old cat softly stalks her in its socks, demanding revenge for its own stolen life.

Even so. The woman who's coldly scheming to . . . in tears over . . . Let's not spell it out.

'Cats can be a bloody nuisance,' Claude says with an air of helpfulness. 'Sharpening their claws on the furniture. But.'

He has nothing antithetical to add. We wait until she's cried herself dry. Then, time for a refill. Why not? A couple of slugs, a neutralising pause, then he rustles in his bag again, and a different vintage is in his hands. A gentler sound as he sets it down. The bottle is plastic.

This time Trudy reads the label but not aloud. 'In summer?'

'Antifreeze contains ethylene glycol, rather good stuff. I treated a neighbour's dog with it once, oversized Alsatian, drove me mad, barking night and day. Anyway. No colour, no smell, pleasant taste, rather sweet, just the thing in a smoothie. Erm. Wrecks the kidneys, excruciating pain. Tiny sharp crystals slice the cells apart. He'll stagger and slur like a drunk, but no smell of alcohol. Nausea, vomiting, hyperventilation, seizures,

50

heart attack, coma, kidney failure. Curtains. Takes a while, as long as someone doesn't mess things up with treatment.'

'Leaves a trace?'

'Everything leaves a trace. You have to consider the advantages. Easy to get hold of, even in summer. Carpet cleaner does the job but doesn't taste as nice. A joy to administer. Goes down a treat. We just need to disassociate you from the moment when it does.'

'Me? What about you?'

'Don't you worry. I'll be disassociated.'

That wasn't what my mother meant, but she lets it pass.

SIX

TRUDY AND I ARE getting drunk again and feeling better, while Claude, starting later with greater body mass, has ground to cover. She and I share two glasses of the Sancerre, he drinks the rest, then returns to his plastic bag for a burgundy. The grey plastic bottle of glycol stands next to the empty, sentinel to our revels. Or memento mori. After a piercing white, a Pinot Noir is a mother's soothing hand. Oh, to be alive while such a grape exists! A blossom, a bouquet of peace and reason. No one seems to want to read aloud the label so I'm forced to make a guess, and hazard an Échézeaux Grand Cru. Put Claude's penis or, less stressful, a gun to my head to name the domaine, I would blurt out la Romanée-Conti, for the spicy cassis and black cherry alone. The hint of violets and fine tannins suggest that lazy, clement summer of 2005, untainted by heatwaves, though a teasing, next-room aroma of mocha, as well as more proximal black-skinned banana, summon Jean Grivot's domaine in 2009. But I'll never know. As the brooding ensemble of flavours, formed at civilisation's summit, makes its way to me, through me, I find myself, in the midst of horror, in reflective mood.

I begin to suspect that my helplessness is not transient. Grant me all the agency the human frame can bear, retrieve my young panther-self of sculpted muscle and long cold stare, direct him to the most extreme measure – killing his uncle to save his father. Put a weapon in his hand, a tyre wrench, a frozen leg of lamb, have him stand behind his uncle's chair, where he can see the anti-freeze and be hotly incited. Ask yourself, could he – could I – do it, smash that hairy knob of bone and spill its grey contents across the squalor of the table? Then murder his mother as sole witness, dispose of two bodies in a basement kitchen, a task only achieved in dreams? And later, clean up that kitchen – another impossible task? Add the prospect of prison, of crazed boredom and the hell of other people, and not the best people. Your even stronger cellmate wants daytime TV all day for thirty years. Care to disoblige him? Then watch him fill a yellowed pillowcase with rocks and slowly turn his gaze your way, towards your own knob of bone.

Or assume the worst, the deed is done – my father's last kidney cells are sheared by a crystal of poison. He's thrown up his lungs and heart into his lap. Agony then coma then death. How about revenge? My avatar shrugs and reaches for his coat, murmuring on his way out that honour killing has no place in the modern polis. Let him speak for himself.

'Seizing the law into your own hands – it's old hat, reserved for elderly feuding Albanians and subsections of tribal Islam. Revenge is dead. Hobbes was right, my young friend. The state must have a monopoly of violence, a common power to keep us all in awe.'

'Then, kind avatar, phone Leviathan now, call the police, make them investigate.'

'What exactly? Claude and Trudy's black humour?'

Constable: 'And this glycol on the table, madam?'

'A plumber suggested it, officer, to keep our ancient radiators unfrozen in winter.'

'Then, dear future best self, get yourself to Shoreditch, warn my father, tell him everything you know.'

'The woman he loves and reveres planning to murder him? How did I come by such information? Was I party to pillow talk, was I under the bed?'

Thus the ideal form of powerful, competent being. What then are my chances, a blind, dumb invert, an almost-child, still living at home, secured by apron strings of arterial and venous blood to the would-be murderess?

But shush! The conspirators are talking.

'It's no bad thing,' says Claude, 'that he's keen to move back here. Put up a show of resistance, then let him come.'

'Oh yes,' she says, cold and satirical. 'And make him a welcome smoothie.'

'I didn't say that. But.'

But I think he almost did.

They pause for thought. My mother reaches for her wine. Her epiglottis stickily rises and falls as she drinks, and the fluid sluices down through her natural alleys, passing – as so much does – near the soles of my feet, curving inwards, heading my way. How can I dislike her?

She sets down her glass and says, 'We can't have him dying here.'

She speaks so easily of his death.

'You're right. Shoreditch is better. You could visit him.'

'And take round a bottle of vintage antifreeze for old times' sake!'

'You take a picnic. Smoked salmon, coleslaw, chocolate fingers. And . . . the business.'

'Haaargh!' Hard to render the sound of my mother's explosive scepticism. 'I dump him, throw him out of his house, take a lover. Then bring him a picnic!'

Even I appreciate my uncle's umbrage at 'take a lover' – as in, one of nameless many, of many yet to come. And it's the 'take', it's the 'a'. Poor fellow. He's only trying to help. He's sitting across from a beautiful young woman with golden braids, in bikini top and cut-offs in a sweltering kitchen, and she's a swollen, gorgeous fruit, a prize he can't bear to lose.

'No,' he says with great care. The affront to his self-regard has pitched his voice higher. 'It's a reconciliation. You're making *amends*. Asking him back. Getting together. Peace offering sort of thing, moment to celebrate, spread out the tablecloth. Get happy!'

Her silence is his reward. She's thinking. As am I. Same old question. Just how stupid is Claude really?

Encouraged, he adds, 'Fruit salad's an option.'

There's poetry in his blandness, a form of nihilism enlivening the commonplace. Or, conversely, the ordinary disarming the vilest notion. Only he could top this, and he does after a thoughtful five seconds.

'Ice cream being out of the question.'

Plain sense. Worth saying. Who would or could make ice cream out of antifreeze?

Trudy sighs. She says in a whisper, 'You know, Claude, I loved him once.'

Is he seeing her as I imagine her? The green gaze is glazing over and, yet again, an early tear is smoothly traversing her cheekbone. Her skin is damply pink, fine hairs have sprung free of her braids and are backlit into brilliant filaments by the ceiling lights.

'We were too young when we met. I mean, we met too soon. On an athletic track. He was throwing the javelin for his club and broke some local record. It made my knees go weak to watch him, the way he ran with that spear. Like a Greek god. A week later he took me

56

to Dubrovnik. We didn't even have a balcony. They say it's a beautiful city.'

I hear the uneasy creak of a kitchen chair. Claude sees the room-service trays piled outside the door, the cloying bedroom's disordered sheets, the nineteen-year-old near-naked at a painted plywood dressing table, her perfect back, a wash-thinned hotel towel across her lap – a parting nod at decency. John Cairncross is jealously excluded, primly out of shot, but huge, and naked too.

Careless of her lover's silence, Trudy hurries on a rising note, before her tightening throat can silence her. 'Trying for a baby all those years. Then just as, just as . . .'

Just as! Worthless adverbial trinket! By the time she tired of my father and his poetry, I was too well lodged to be unhoused. She cries now for John as she did for Hector the cat. Perhaps my mother's nature won't stretch to a second killing.

'Erm,' Claude says at last, offering his crumb. 'Spilt milk and all.'

Milk, repellent to the blood-fed unborn, especially after wine, but my future all the same.

He waits patiently to present his idea of a picnic. It can't help, to hear his rival wept for. Or perhaps it concentrates the mind. He drums his fingers lightly on the table, one of the things he does. When standing he

57

rattles his house keys in his trouser pocket, or unproductively clears his throat. These empty gestures, devoid of self-awareness, are sinister. There's a whiff of sulphur about Claude. But for the moment we're as one, for I'm waiting too, troubled by a sickly fascination to know his scheme, as one might the ending of a play. He can hardly expound while she's weeping.

A minute later she blows her nose and says in a croaky voice, 'Anyway, I hate him now.'

'He made you very unhappy.'

She nods and blows her nose again. Now we listen while he presents his verbal brochure. His delivery is that of the doorstep evangelist helping her towards a better life. Essential, he tells us, that my mother and I make at least one visit to Shoreditch before the last, fatal call. Hopeless to conceal from forensics that she was ever there. Helpful to establish that she and John were on terms again.

This, he says, must look like suicide, like Cairncross made a cocktail for himself to improve the poison's taste. Therefore, on her final visit she'll leave behind the original empty bottles of glycol and shop-bought smoothie. These vessels must show no trace of her fingerprints. She'll need to wax her fingertips. He has just the stuff. Bloody good too. Before she leaves John's flat, she'll put the picnic remains inside the fridge. Any containers or wrapping must also be free of her prints. It should seem as though he ate alone. As beneficiary of his will, she'll be investigated, a conspiracy suspected. So all traces of Claude, in bedroom and bathroom especially, must be eradicated, cleaned to extinction, every last hair and flake of skin. And, I sense her thinking, every no-longer thrashing tail, every stilled head of every last sperm. That may take some time.

Claude continues. No concealing the phone calls she has made to him. The phone company will have a record.

'But remember. I'm just a friend.'

It costs him to say these last words, especially when my mother repeats them as in a catechism. Words, as I'm beginning to appreciate, can make things true.

'You're just my friend.'

'Yes. Called round from time to time. For a chat. Brother-in-law. Helping you out. Nothing more.'

His account has been neutrally rendered, as though he daily murders brothers, husbands for a living, an honest high-street butcher by trade whose bloody apron mixes in the family wash with the sheets and towels.

Trudy starts to say, 'But listen—' when Claude cuts her off with a sudden remembered thought.

'Did you see? A house in our street, same side, same size, same condition? On the market for *eight* million!'

My mother absorbs this in silence. It's the 'our' she's taking in.

There it is. We've made another million by not

killing my father sooner. How true it is: we make our own luck. But. (As Claude would say.) I don't know much yet about murder. Still, his scheme is more baker than butcher. Half-baked. The absence of prints on the glycol bottle will be suspicious. When my father starts to feel ill, what stops him calling the emergency services? They'll pump his stomach. He'll be fine. Then what?

'I don't care about house prices,' Trudy says. 'That's for later. The bigger question is this. Where's your risk, what's your exposure here when you're wanting a share of the money? If something goes wrong and I go down, where will you be once I've scrubbed you out of my bedroom?'

I'm surprised by her bluntness. And then I experience not quite joy, but its expectation, a cool uncoiling in my gut. A falling out among villains, the already useless plot ruined, my father saved.

'Trudy, I'll be with you at every step.'

'You'll be safe at home. Alibis in place. Perfect deniability.'

She's been thinking about this. Thinking without my knowing. She's a tigress.

Claude says. 'The thing is—'

'What I want,' my mother says with a vehemence that hardens the walls around me, 'is you tied into this, and I mean totally. If I fail, you fail. If I—'

The doorbell rings once, twice, three times, and we

freeze. No one, in my experience, has ever come to the front door so late. Claude's plan is so hopeless it's failed already, for here are the police. No one else rings a bell with such dogged insistence. The kitchen was bugged long ago, they've heard it all. Trudy will have her way – we'll all go down together. *Babies Behind Bars* was a too-long radio documentary I listened to one afternoon. Convicted murderers in the States, nursing mothers, were allowed to raise their infants in their cells. This was presented as an enlightened development. But I remember thinking, These babies have done nothing wrong. Set them free! Ah well. Only in America.

'I'll go.'

He gets up and crosses the room to the video entry-phone on the wall by the kitchen door. He peers at the screen.

'It's your husband,' he says dully.

'Jesus.' My mother pauses to think. 'No use pretending I'm not here. You better hide somewhere. In the laundry room. He never—'

'There's someone with him. A woman. A young woman. Rather pretty, I'd say.'

Another silence. The bell rings again. Longer.

My mother's voice is even, though strained. 'In that case, go and let them in. But Claude, darling. Kindly put that glycol bottle away.'

61

CERTAIN ARTISTS IN PRINT or paint flourish, like babies-to-be, in confined spaces. Their narrow subjects may confound or disappoint some. Courtship among the eighteenth-century gentry, life beneath the sail, talking rabbits, sculpted hares, fat people in oils, dog portraits, horse portraits, portraits of aristocrats, reclining nudes, Nativities by the million, and Crucifixions, Assumptions, bowls of fruit, flowers in vases. And Dutch bread and cheese with or without a knife on the side. Some give themselves in prose merely to the self. In science too, one dedicates his life to an Albanian snail, another to a virus. Darwin gave eight years to barnacles. And in wise later life, to earthworms. The Higgs boson, a tiny thing, perhaps not even a thing, was the lifetime's pursuit of thousands. To be bound in a nutshell, see the world in two inches of ivory, in a grain of sand. Why not, when all of literature, all of art, of human endeavour, is just a speck in the universe of possible things. And even this universe may be a speck in a multitude of actual and possible universes.

So why not be an owl poet?

I know them by their footfalls. First down the open stairs to the kitchen comes Claude, then my father, followed by his newly signed-up friend, in high heels, boots perhaps, not ideal for stalking through woodland habitats. By nocturnal association I dress her in tight-fitting black leather jacket and jeans, let her be young, pale, pretty, her own woman. My placenta, like branching radio antennae, finely attuned, is receiving signals that my mother instantly detests her. Unreasonable thoughts are disrupting Trudy's pulse, a new and ominous drum-beat rising as though from a distant jungle village speaks of possession, anger, jealousy. There could be trouble ahead.

I feel obliged for my father's sake to defend our visitor: her subject is not so limited, owls being larger than bosons or barnacles, with two hundred species and wide folklorique resonance. Mostly of ill-omen. Unlike Trudy, with her visceral certainties, I quiver with doubts. Either my father, being neither sap nor saint, has come to present his lover, put my mother in her place (which is in his past) and show indifference to his brother's infamy. Or he's even more the sap, too much the saint, dropping in chastely with one of his authors as a form of social protection, in hopes of being in Trudy's presence for as long as she'll tolerate him. Or something beyond both, too opaque to determine. Simpler, for now at least, to follow my mother's lead and assume that this friend is my father's mistress.

No child, still less a foetus, has ever mastered the art

of small talk, or would ever want to. It's an adult device, a covenant with boredom and deceit. In this case mostly the latter. After a tentative scrape of chairs, the offer of wine, the pull of a cork, a comment from Claude about the heat draws my father's neutral hum of assent. A fitful exchange between the brothers projects the lie that our visitors happened to be passing. Trudy remains silent, even when the poet is introduced as Elodie. No one comments on the elegant social geometry of a married couple and their lovers around a table, raising a glass, a *tableau vivant* of brittle modern life.

My father appears unfazed to find his brother in his kitchen, opening the wine, playing the host. So John Cairncross was never the dupe, the unknowing cuckold. My underestimated father blandly sips and asks Trudy how she's feeling. Not too tired, he hopes. Which may or may not be a gentle dig, a sexual allusion. That plaintive tone of his has vanished. Distance or irony has replaced it. Only satisfied desire could have freed him. Trudy and Claude must wonder why their murderee is here, what he wants, but it wouldn't be right to ask.

Instead, Claude asks Elodie if she lives nearby. No, she doesn't. She lives in Devon, in a studio, on a farm, near a river, by which she might be letting Trudy know that here in London she'll be overnighting between John's Shoreditch sheets. She's staking a claim. I like the sound of her voice, the human approximation, I would say, of the oboe, slightly cracked, with a quack on the vowels. And towards the end of her phrases, she speaks through a gargling, growling sound that American linguists have dubbed 'vocal fry'. Spreading through the Western world, much discussed on the radio, of unknown aetiology, signifying, it's thought, sophistication, found mostly in young, educated women. A pleasing puzzle. With such a voice she might hold her own against my mother.

Nothing in my father's manner suggests that only this afternoon his brother fronted him five thousand pounds in cash. No gratitude, same old fraternal contempt. That must stir Claude's ancient hatred. And in me, something more hypothetical, a *potential* grudge. Even as I cast my father as a lovelorn fool, I always assumed that if matters became intolerable with Claude, and if I failed to unite my parents, I might live with my father, at least for a while. Until I got on my feet. But I don't think this poet would take me on – tight black jeans and leather jacket is not maternity wear. That's part of her allure. In my narrow view, my father would be better single. Pale beauty and an assured duck's voice are not my allies. But there may be nothing between them, and I like her.

Claude has just said, 'A studio? On a farm? How marvellous.' Elodie is describing in her urban growl an A-frame cabin on the banks of a dark and rushing river that foams round granite boulders, a dodgy footbridge to the other side, a copse of beeches and birch, a bright clearing spangled with anemones and celandines, bluebells and spurge.

'Perfect for a nature poet,' Claude says.

So true and dull is this that Elodie falters. He presses in. 'How far is it all from London?'

By 'all' he refers to the pointless river and rocks and trees and flowers. Deflated, she can barely fry her words. 'About two hundred miles.'

She's guessed that he'll ask her about the nearest railway station and how long the journey takes, information he'll soon forget. But he asks, she answers, and we three listen, not stupefied or even mildly bored. Each of us, from each different point of view, is gripped by what's not being said. The lovers, if Elodie is one, the two parties external to the marriage, are the dual charge that will blast this household apart. And blow me upwards, hellwards, to my thirteenth floor.

In a gentle tone of rescue, John Cairncross mentions that he likes the wine, a prompt to Claude to refill the glasses. While he obliges there settles over us a silence. I conjure a taut piano wire waiting for its sudden felt hammer. Trudy is about to speak. I know from the syncopated trip of her heartbeat, just before her first word.

'These owls. Are they real or do they, like, stand for something?'

'Oh no,' Elodie says in a rush. 'They're real. I write

from life. But the reader, you know, *imports* the symbols, the associations. I can't keep them out. That's how poetry works.'

'I always think of owls,' says Claude, 'as wise.'

The poet pauses, tasting the air for sarcasm. She's getting his measure and says evenly, 'There you are then. Nothing I can do about that.'

'Owls are vicious,' Trudy says.

Elodie: 'Like robins are. Like nature is.'

Trudy: 'Inedible, apparently.'

Elodie: 'And the broody owl is poisonous.'

Trudy: 'Yes, the broody one can kill you.'

Elodie: 'I don't think so. She just makes you sick.'

Trudy: 'I mean, if she gets her claws into your face.'

Elodie: 'Never happens. She's too shy.'

Trudy: 'Not when provoked.'

The exchange is relaxed, the tone inconsequential. Small talk or a trade in threat and insult – I lack the social experience to know. If I'm drunk then Trudy must be too, but there's nothing in her manner to suggest it. Loathing for Elodie, now framed as a rival, may be an elixir of sobriety.

John Cairncross seems content to pass his wife on to Claude Cairncross. This puts the steel in my mother, who believes the discarding and passing on is *hers* to decide. She may deny my father Elodie. She may deny him life itself. But I may be wrong. My father reciting in the library, appearing to prize every second in my mother's presence, allowing her to shove him into the street.(*Just go!*) I can't trust my judgement. Nothing fits.

But no time to think now. He's on his feet, looming over us, wine in hand, swaying barely at all, ready to make a speech. Quiet everyone.

'Trudy, Claude, Elodie, I might be brief, I might not. Who cares? I want to say this. When love dies and a marriage lies in ruins, the first casualty is honest memory, decent, impartial recall of the past. Too inconvenient, too damning of the present. It's the spectre of old happiness at the feast of failure and desolation. So, against that headwind of forgetfulness I want to place my little candle of truth and see how far it throws its light. Almost ten years ago, on the Dalmatian coast, in a cheap hotel without sight of the Adriatic, in a room an eighth the size of this, in a bed barely three feet across, Trudy and I tumbled into love, into ecstasy and trust, joy and peace without horizon, without time, beyond words. We turned our backs on the world to invent and build our own. We thrilled each other with pretended violence, and we cosseted and babied each other too, gave each other nick-names, had a private language. We were beyond embarrassment. We gave and received and permitted everything. We were heroic. We believed we stood on a summit no one else, not in life, not in all poetry, had ever climbed. Our love was so fine and grand, it seemed to us

68

a universal principle. It was a system of ethics, a means of relating to others that was so fundamental that the world had overlooked it somehow. When we lay on the narrow bed face to face, looked deep into each other's eyes and talked, we brought our selves into being. She took my hands and kissed them and for the first time in my life I wasn't ashamed of them. Our families, which we described to each other in detail, at last made sense to us. We loved them urgently, despite all the difficulties of the past. Same with our best, most important friends. We could redeem everyone we knew. Our love was for the good of the world. Trudy and I had never talked or listened with such attention. Our lovemaking was an extension of our talking, our talking of our lovemaking.

'When that week was over and we came back and set up together here in my house, the love went on, months then years. It seemed that nothing could ever get in its way. So before I go any further, I'm raising my glass to that love. May it never be denied, forgotten, distorted or rejected as illusion. To our love. It happened. It was true.'

I hear a shuffle and murmur of reluctant accord and, closer by, I hear my mother swallow hard before she pretends to drink the toast. I think she's taken against 'my house'.

'Now,' my father continues, lowering his voice, as though entering a funeral parlour, 'that love has run its course. It never collapsed into mere routine or a hedge against old age. It died quickly, tragically, as love on a grand scale must. The curtain's come down. It's over, and I'm glad. Trudy's glad. Everyone who knows us is glad and relieved. We trusted each other, now we don't. We loved each other, now I detest her as much as she detests me. Trudy, my sweet, I can hardly stand the sight of you. There have been times when I could have strangled you. I've had dreams, happy dreams, in which I see my thumbs tightening against your carotid arteries. I know you feel the same about me. But that's no cause for regret. Let's rejoice instead. These are just the dark feelings we need to set ourselves free, to be reborn into new life and new love. Elodie and I have found that love and we are bound by it for the rest of our lives.'

'Wait,' Elodie says. I think she fears my father's taste for indiscretion.

But he won't take an interruption. 'Trudy and Claude, I'm happy for you. You came together at the perfect moment. No one will deny it, you truly deserve each other.'

This is a curse, though my father sounds impenetrably sincere. To be tied to a man as vapid but sexually vigorous as Claude is a complex fate. His brother knows it. But shush. He's still talking.

'There are arrangements to make. There'll be arguments and stress. But the overall scheme is simple, and for that we're blessed. Claude, you have your nice big place in Primrose Hill, and Trudy, you can move there. I'll be moving some stuff back in here tomorrow. As soon as you've gone and the decorators have done their work, Elodie will move in with me. I suggest we don't see each other for a year or so, and then think again. The divorce should be straightforward. The important thing to remember at all times is to be rational and civil and to remember how lucky we are to have found love again. OK? Good. No, no, don't get up. We'll see ourselves out. Trudy, if you're here, I'll see you tomorrow around ten. I won't stay long – I've got to get straight up to St Albans. And by the way, I've found my key.'

There's the sound of a chair as Elodie stands. 'Wait, I mean, may I say something now?'

My father is genial and firm. 'Not remotely appropriate.'

'But—'

'C'mon. Time to go. Thanks for the wine.'

A moment of throat-clearing, then their footsteps recede across the kitchen and up the stairs.

My mother and her lover sit in silence as we listen to them go. We hear the front door close upstairs with a punctuating, final sound. A full stop. Trudy and Claude are stunned. I'm in turmoil. What was I in my father's peroration? Dead. Head-first in a burial mound within his hated ex-wife's gut. Not even a mention, not in an aside, not even dismissed as an irrelevance. A year 'or so' must pass before my saviour sees me. He paid tribute to honest memory and he forgot me. In a rush towards his own rebirth, he discarded mine. Fathers and sons. I heard it once and won't forget. *What links them in nature? An instant of blind rut.*

Try this. He moved to Shoreditch to sample a tryst with Elodie. He vacated the Terrace so Claude could move in and give John good cause to throw Trudy out. The anxious visits, the earnest poetry, even the lost key were feints, lulling her into greater security with Claude, drawing them together.

Claude is pouring more wine. In the circumstances it's a comfort, how he reaches with dull precision for his most vacuous thought.

'Fancy that.'

Trudy doesn't speak for half a minute. When she does, her words are slurred but her resolve is clear.

'I want him dead. And it has to be tomorrow.'

EIGHT

OUTSIDE THESE WARM, LIVING walls an icy tale slides towards its hideous conclusion. The midsummer clouds are thick, there's no moon, not the faintest breeze. But my mother and uncle are talking up a winter storm. The cork is drawn from one more bottle, then, too soon, another. I'm washed far downstream of drunkenness, my senses blur their words but I hear in them the form of my ruin. Shadow figures on a bloody screen are arguing in hopeless struggle with their fate. The voices rise and fall. When they don't accuse or wrangle, they conspire. What's said hangs in the air, like a Beijing smog.

It will end badly, and the house feels the ruin too. In high summer, the February gale twists and breaks the icicles hanging from the gutters, scours the unpointed brickwork of the gable ends, rips the slates – those blank slates – from the pitching roofs. This chill works its fingers past the rotted putty of the unwashed panes, it backs up through the kitchen drains. I'm shivering in here. But it won't end, the bad will be endless, until ending badly will seem a blessing. Nothing will be forgotten, nothing flushed away. Foul matter lingers in unseen bends beyond the plumber's reach, it hangs in the wardrobes with

Trudy's winter coats. This too solid stench feeds the timid mice behind the skirting and swells them to rats. We hear their gnawing and mutinous curses, but no one is surprised. At intervals, my mother and I retire so she may squat and copiously piss and groan. Against my skull I feel her bladder shrink, and I'm relieved. Back to the table, to more scheming and long harangues. It was my uncle cursing, not the rats. That gnawing was my mother at the salted nuts. Incessantly, she eats for me.

In here, I dream of my entitlement – security, weightless peace, no tasks, no crime or guilt. I'm thinking about what should have been mine in my confinement. Two opposing notions haunt me. I heard about them in a podcast my mother left running while talking on the phone. We were on the couch in my father's library, windows wide open to another sultry midday. Boredom, said this Monsieur Barthes, is not far from bliss; one regards boredom from the shores of pleasure. Exactly so. The condition of the modern foetus. Just think: nothing to do but be and grow, where growing is hardly a conscious act. The joy of pure existence, the tedium of undifferentiated days. Extended bliss is boredom of the existential kind. This confinement shouldn't be a prison. In here I'm owed the privilege and luxury of solitude. I speak as an innocent, but I conjure an orgasm prolonged into eternity – there's boredom for you, in the realm of the sublime.

This was my patrimony, until my mother wished

my father dead. Now I live inside a story and fret about its outcome. Where's boredom or bliss in that?

My uncle rises from the kitchen table, lurches towards the wall to turn off the lights and reveal the dawn. If he'd been my father, he might have recited an aubade. But now there's only a practical concern – it's time for bed. What deliverance, that they're too drunk for sex. Trudy stands, together we sway. If I could be upright for one minute I'd feel less sick. How I miss my spacious days of ocean-tumbling.

With one foot on the first tread, she halts to gauge the climb ahead. It rises severely and recedes, as though to the moon. I feel her grip the banister on my account. I still love her, I'd like her to know, but if she falls backwards, I die. Now we're going mostly up. Mostly, Claude is ahead of us. We should be roped. Grip tighter, Mother! It's an effort and no one speaks. After many minutes, many sighs and moans, we gain the second-floor landing, and the rest, the last twelve feet, though level, is also tough.

She sits on her side of the bed to remove a sandal, topples sideways with it in her hand, and falls asleep. Claude shakes her awake. Together they fumble in the bathroom, through the spilling drawers, in search of two grams each of paracetamol, a means to hold a hangover at bay.

Claude notes, 'Tomorrow's a busy day.'

He means today. My father is due at ten, now it's almost six. Finally, we're all in bed. My mother complains that the world, her world, spins when she closes her eyes. I thought Claude might be more stoical, made, as he might say, of sterner stuff. Not so. Within minutes he's hurried next door to fall to his knees and embrace the lavatory bowl.

'Lift the seat,' Trudy shouts.

Silence, then it comes, in hard-won dribbles. But he's loud. A long shout truncated, as though a football fan has been stabbed in the back mid-chant.

By seven they're asleep. Not me. My thoughts turn with my mother's world. My father's rejection of me, his possible fate, my responsibility for it, then my own fate, my inability to warn or act. And my bedfellows. Too damaged to make the attempt? Or worse, to do it badly, be caught and sent down. Hence the spectral prison that's lately haunted me. To start life in a cell, bliss unknown, boredom a fought-for privilege. And if they succeed – then it's the Vale of Swat. I see no scheme, no plausible route to any conceivable happiness. I wish never to be born . . .

* * *

I overslept. I'm woken by a shout and a violent, arrhythmic jigging. My mother on the Wall of Death.

Not so. Or not that one. This is her descending the stairs too fast, her careless hand barely trailing the banister. Here's how it could end, the loose carpet rod or curling threadbare carpet edge, the head-first downward pitch, then my private gloom lost to eternal darkness. I've nothing to hold on to but hope. The shout was from my uncle. He calls out again.

'I've been out for the drink. We've got twenty minutes. Make the coffee. I'll do the rest.'

His dim Shoreditch plans have been ditched by my mother's lust for speed. John Cairncross is not her fool after all. He'll kick her out, and soon. She must act today. No time to tend her plaits. She's given hospitality to her husband's lover – dumped before she could dump, as they say on the afternoon agony-aunt shows. (Teenagers phone in with problems that would stump a Plato or a Kant.) Trudy's anger is oceanic – vast and deep, it's her medium, her selfhood. I know it in her altered blood as it washes through me, in the granular discomfort where cells are bothered and compressed, the platelets cracked and chipped. My heart is struggling with my mother's angry blood.

We're safely on the ground floor, among the busy morning hum of flies that cruise the hallway's garbage. To them the untied plastic bags rise like shining residential towers with rooftop gardens. The flies go there to graze and vomit at their ease. Their general bloated laziness invokes a society of mellow recreation, communal purpose, mutual tolerance. This somnolent, non-chordate crew is at one with the world, it loves rich life in all its putrefaction. Whereas we're a lower form, fearful and in constant discord. We've got the jitters, we're going too fast.

Trudy's trailing hand grips the newel post and we swing through a speedy U-turn. Ten steps and we're at the head of the kitchen stairs. No handrail to guide us down. It fell off the wall, I heard, in a burst of dust and horsehair, before my time, if this is my time. Only irregular holes remain. The treads are bare pine, with slick and greasy knots, palimpsests of forgotten spills, downtrodden meat and fat, and molten butter sliding off the toast my father used to carry to the library without a plate. Again, she's going at speed, and this could be it, the headlong launch. Hardly has the thought illuminated my fears when I sense a backwards-sliding foot, a forward lurch, an urge to flight, countered at once by a panicky tightening of the muscles in her lower back and from behind my shoulder I hear a wrenching sound of tendons stretching and testing their anchors on the bone.

'My back,' she growls. 'My fucking back.'

But it's worth her pain, for she's steadied herself and takes the remaining steps with care. Claude, busy by the kitchen sink, pauses to make a sympathetic sound, then continues with his tasks. Time waits for no man, as he might say.

She's at his side. 'My head,' she whispers.

'And mine.' Then he shows her. 'I think it's his favourite. Bananas, pineapple, apple, mint, wheat germ.'

'Tropical Dawn?'

'Yup. And here's the business. Enough to fell ten ox.'

'Oxen.'

He pours the two liquids into the blender and activates it.

When the din has ceased she says, 'Put it in the fridge. I'll make the coffee. Hide those paper cups. Don't touch them without your gloves.'

We're at the coffee machine. She's found the filters, she's spooning in the grains, tipping in the water. Doing well.

'Wash some mugs,' she calls. 'And set them out. Get the stuff ready for the car. John's gloves are in the outhouse. They'll need dusting down. And there's a plastic bag somewhere.'

'All right, all right.' Out of bed long before her, Claude sounds testy as she takes control. I struggle to follow their exchange.

'My thing and the bank statement are on the table.'

'I know.'

'Don't forget the receipt.'

'I won't.

'Screw it up a bit.'

'I have.'

'With your gloves. Not his.'

'Yes!'

'You wore the hat in Judd Street?'

'Of course.'

'Put it where he'll see it.'

'I *have.*'

But he's at the sink, rinsing crusty cups, doing as he's told. She's impervious to his tone and adds, 'We should tidy this place up.'

He grunts. A hopeless notion. Good wife Trudy wants to greet her husband with a tidy kitchen.

But surely none of this can work. Elodie knows that my father is expected here. Perhaps half a dozen friends know too. London, north to east, will point a finger across the corpse. Here's a pretty *folie à deux*. Could my mother, who's never had a job, launch herself as a murderer? A tough profession, not only in the planning and execution, but in the aftermath, when the career would properly begin. Consider, I want to say to her, even before the ethics, the inconvenience: imprisonment or guilt or both, extended hours, weekends too, and all through every night, for life. No pay, no perks, no pension but remorse. She's making a mistake.

But the lovers are locked in, as only lovers can be.

Being busy about the kitchen keeps them steady. They clear from the table last night's debris, sweep up or sweep aside food scraps on the floor, then down more pain-killers with a slug of coffee. That's all the breakfast I'm getting. They agree that around the kitchen sink there's nothing to be done. My mother mutters instructions, or guidelines. Claude remains terse. Each time, he cuts her off. He may be having second thoughts.

'Cheerful, OK? Like we thought through what he said last night and decided—'

'Right.'

After minutes of silence: 'Don't go offering too soon. We need—'

'I won't.'

And again: 'Two empty glasses to show that we've had some ourselves already. And the Smoothie Heaven cup—'

'It's done. They're behind you.'

On his final word we're startled by my father's voice from the top of the kitchen stairs. Of course, he has his key. He's in the house.

He calls down. 'Just unloading the car. Then I'll be with you.'

His tone is gruff, competent. Unearthly love has made him worldly.

Claude whispers, 'What if he locks it?'

I'm close to my mother's heart and know its rhythms

and sudden turns. And now! It accelerates at her husband's voice, and there's an added sound, a disturbance in the chambers, like the distant rattling of maracas, or gravel shuffled softly in a tin. From down here I'd say it's a semilunar valve whose cusps are snapping shut too hard and sticking. Or it could be her teeth.

But to the world my mother appears serene. She remains the liege and mistress of her voice, which is even and doesn't stoop to whispers.

'He's a poet. He never locks the car. When I give you the sign, go out there with the stuff.'

NINE

Dear Father,

Before you die, I'd like a word. We haven't much time. Far less than you think, so forgive me for coming to the point. I need to tap your memory. There was a morning in your library, a Sunday of unusual summer rain when the air for once was clean of dust. The windows were open, we heard the pattering on the leaves. You and my mother almost resembled a happy couple. There was a poem you recited then, too good for one of yours, I think you'd be the first to concede. Short, dense, bitter to the point of resignation, difficult to understand. The sort that hits you, hurts you, before you've followed exactly what was said. It addressed a careless, indifferent reader, a lost lover, a real person, I should think. In fourteen lines it talked of hopeless attachment, wretched preoccupation, longing unresolved and unacknowledged. It summoned a rival, mighty in talent or social rank or both, and it bowed in self-effacement. Eventually, time would have its revenge, but no one would care or even remember, unless they chanced to read these lines.

The person the poem addressed I think of as the world I'm about to meet. Already, I love it too hard. I don't know what it will make of me, whether it will care for me or even notice me. From here it seems unkind, careless of life, of lives. The news is brutal, unreal, a nightmare we can't wake from. I listen with my mother, rapt and glum. Enslaved teenage girls, prayed over then raped. Barrels used as bombs over cities, children used as bombs in marketplaces. We heard from Austria about a locked roadside truck and seventy-one migrants left to panic, suffocate and rot. Only the brave would send their imaginations inside the final moments. These are new times. Perhaps they're ancient. But also, that poem makes me think of you and your speech last night and how you won't or can't return my love. From where I am, you and my mother and the world are all one. Hyperbole, I know. The world is also full of wonders, which is why I'm foolishly in love with it. And I love and admire you both. What I'm saying is, I'm fearful of rejection.

So say it again to me, this poem, with your dying breath and I'll say it back to you. Let it be the last thing you ever hear. Then you'll know what I mean. Or take the kinder course, live rather than die, accept your son, hold me in your arms, claim me for your own. In return I'll give you some advice. Don't come down the stairs. Call out a carefree goodbye, get in your car and go. Or if you must come down, decline the fruit drink, stay only long enough to say your farewells. I'll explain later. Until then, I remain your obedient son . . .

We're sitting at the kitchen table, attending in silence to the intermittent thumps of my father's footfalls above as he brings in boxes of books and leaves them in the sitting room. Murderers before the deed find small talk a burden. Dry mouth, thready pulse, whirling thoughts. Even Claude is stumped. He and Trudy drink more black coffee. At each mouthful they put their cups down without a sound. They're not using saucers. There's a clock I haven't noticed before, ticking in thoughtful iambs. Along the street, a delivery van's pop music approaches and recedes with a faint Doppler effect, the cheerless band lifting and dipping a microtone but staying in tune with itself. There's a message in there for me, just out of reach. The painkillers are coming on, but the gain is mere clarity where numbness would suit me better. They've been through it twice and everything is in order. The cups, the potion, the 'thing', something from the bank, the hat and gloves and receipt, the plastic bag. I'm baffled. I should have listened last night. I won't know if the plan is going well or about to unravel.

'I could go up and help him,' Claude says at last. 'You know, many hands make—'

'OK, OK. Wait.' My mother can't bear to hear the rest. She and I have much in common.

We hear the front door close, and seconds later those same shoes – old-style leather soles – making the sound on the stairs they made last night when he came down with his lover and settled his fate. He whistles tunelessly as he comes, more Schoenberg than Schubert, a projection of ease rather than the thing itself. Nervous then, despite the lordly speech. No easy matter, to evict your brother and the woman you hate who bears your child from the house you love. He's nearer now. Again, my ear is stuck to the gluey wall. There's no inflection or pause or swallowed word I'd care to miss.

My informal family dispenses with greetings.

'I was hoping to see your suitcase by the door.' He says it humorously and, as usual, ignores his brother.

'Not a chance,' my mother smoothly says. 'Sit down and have a coffee.'

He sits. A pouring sound, a teaspoon clinks.

Then my father. 'A contractor's coming to remove the appalling mess that's in the hall.'

'It's not a mess. It's a statement.'

'Of what?'

'Protest.'

'Oh yes?'

'At your neglect.'

'Hah!'

'Of me. And our baby.'

This could be in the noble cause of realism, of the plausible. An oily welcome might raise his guard. And recalling him to his paternal duty – brava!

'They'll be here at twelve. Pest control are coming too. They'll be fumigating the place.'

'Not while we're here they won't.'

'That's up to you. They start at midday.'

'They'll have to wait a month or two.'

'I've paid them double to ignore you. And they have a key.'

'Oh,' says Trudy, with an appearance of true regret. 'I'm sorry you've wasted so much money. A poet's money at that.'

Claude leaps in, too soon for Trudy. 'I've made this delicious—'

'Dearest, everyone needs more coffee.'

The man who obliterates my mother between the sheets obeys like a dog. Sex, I begin to understand, is its own mountain kingdom, secret and intact. In the valley below we know only rumours.

As Claude stoops over the machine on the far side of the room, my mother says pleasantly to her husband, 'While we're on it, I hear your brother was very kind to you. Five thousand pounds! Lucky boy. Did you thank him?'

'He'll get it back, if that's what you mean.'

'Like the last lot.'

'He'll get that too.'

'I hate to think of you spending it all on fumigators.'

My father laughs in genuine delight. 'Trudy! I can almost remember why I loved you. By the way, you're looking beautiful.'

'A little unkempt,' she says. 'But thank you.' Theatrically, she lowers her voice, as though to exclude Claude. 'After you left we partied. All night long.'

'Celebrating your eviction.'

'You could say that.'

We lean forward, she and I, me feet first, and my impression is that she's put her hand on his. He's closer now to the sweet disorder of her braids, the wide green look, the pink-perfect skin perfumed with the scent he bought her long ago in the Dubrovnik duty-free. How she thinks ahead.

'We had a glass or two and we talked. We decided. You're right. Time to go our separate ways. Claude's place is nice and St John's Wood is a dump compared to Primrose Hill. And I'm so happy about your new friend. Threnody.'

'Elodie. She's lovely. We had a terrible fight when we got in last night.'

'But you looked so happy together.' I note the lift in my mother's tone.

'She's decided that I'm still in love with you.'

This too has an effect on Trudy. 'But you said it yourself. We hate each other.'

'Quite. She thinks I protest too much.'

'John! Should I phone her? Tell her how much I loathe you?'

His laugh sounds uncertain. 'Now there's the path to perdition!'

I'm recalled to my mission: the sacred, imagined duty of the child of separated parents is to unite them. Perdition. A poet's word. Lost and damned. I'm a fool to let my hopes rise a point or two, like a futures market after a rout and before the next. My parents are merely playing, tickling each other's parts. Elodie is mistaken. What stands between the married pair is no more than protective irony.

Here's Claude bearing a tray, something heavy or sulky in his offer.

'More coffee?'

'God, no,' my father says in the simple, dismissive tone he reserves for his brother.

'We've also got some nice—'

'Darling, I'll have another cup. A big one.'

'Your bro,' my mother says to my uncle, 'is in the doghouse with Threnody.'

'A threnody,' my father defines for her with exaggerated care, 'is a song for the dead.'

'Like "Candle in the Wind",' says Claude, coming to life.

'For God's sake.'

'Anyway,' Trudy says, retreating some steps back through their exchange. 'This is the marital home. I'll move out when I'm ready and it won't be this week.'

'Come on. You know the fumigator was just a tease. But you can't deny it. The place is a shithole.'

'Press me too hard, John, and I might decide to stay. See you in court.'

'Point taken. But you won't mind if we remove the crap in the hall.'

'I do mind a bit.' Then, after a moment's contemplation, she nods her assent.

I hear Claude pick up the plastic bag. His cheeriness wouldn't convince the dimmest child. 'If you'll excuse me. Stuff to do. No rest for the wicked!'

TEN

THERE WAS A TIME when Claude's exit line might have made me smile. But lately, don't ask why, I've no taste for comedy, no inclination to exercise, even if I had the space, no delight in fire or earth, in words that once revealed a golden world of majestical stars, the beauty of poetic apprehension, the infinite joy of reason. These admirable radio talks and bulletins, the excellent podcasts that moved me, seem at best hot air, at worst a vaporous stench. The brave polity I'm soon to join, the noble congregation of humanity, its customs, gods and angels, its fiery ideas and brilliant ferment, no longer thrill me. A weight bears down heavily on the canopy that wraps my little frame. There's hardly enough of me to form one small animal, still less to express a man. My disposition is to stillborn sterility, then to dust.

These lowering, high-flown thoughts, which I long to declaim alone somewhere, return to oppress me as Claude disappears up the stairs and my parents sit in silence. We hear the front door open and close. I strain without success for the sound of Claude opening the door of his brother's car. Trudy leans forward again and John takes her hand. The faintest rise in our blood pressure suggests a squeeze of his psoriatic fingers against her palm. She says his name quietly, with a falling tone of fond reproach. He says nothing, but my best guess is he's shaking his head, compressing his lips into a thin smile, as if to say, Well, well. Look what's come of us.

She says warmly, 'You were right, it's the end. But we can do this gently.'

'Yes, it's best,' my father agrees in his pleasant, rumbling voice. 'But Trudy. Just for old times. Shall I say a poem for you?'

Her emphatic, childlike shake of the head gently rocks me on my bearings, but I know as well as she does that, for John Cairncross, in poetry no means yes.

'Please John, for heaven's sake don't.'

But he's already drawing breath. I've heard this one, but it meant less then.

'Since there's no help, come let us kiss and part . . .'

Unnecessary, I think, for him to be speaking certain phrases with such relish. 'You get no more of me', 'so cleanly I myself can free', not 'one jot of former love retain'. And at the end, when Passion is on his deathbed, and there's a chance against the odds he might recover if only Trudy wished it, my father denies it all with a clever, sarcastic lilt.

But she doesn't wish it either and talks over the last few words. 'I don't want to hear another poem for the rest of my life.'

'You won't,' my father says affably. 'Not with Claude.'

In this sensible exchange between the parties, no provision is made for me. Another man's suspicions would be stirred by his ex-wife's failure to negotiate the monthly payments that must be due to the mother of his child. Another woman, if she didn't have schemes in hand, would surely demand it. But I'm old enough to take responsibility for myself and try to be the master of my fate. Like the miser's cat, I retain a secret scrap of sustenance, my one morsel of agency. I've used it in the small hours to inflict insomnia and summon a radio talk. Two sharp, well-spaced blows against the wall, using my heel rather than my near-boneless toes. I feel it as a lonely pulse of longing, just to hear myself referred to.

'Ah,' my mother sighs. 'He's kicking.'

'Then I should be going,' my father murmurs. 'Shall we say two weeks for you to clear out?'

I wave to him, as it were, and what do I get? Then, therefore, in which case, and so – he's *going*.

'Two months. But hang on a minute till Claude gets back.'

'Only if he's quick.'

An airplane a few thousand feet above our heads makes an airy downward glissando towards Heathrow, a threatening sound, I always think. John Cairncross may be considering one last poem. He could wheel out, as he used to before journeys, 'A Valediction Forbidding Mourning'. Those soothing tetrameters, that mature, comforting tone, would make me nostalgic for the sad old days of his visits. But instead he drums his fingers on the table, clears his throat, and simply waits.

Trudy says, 'We had smoothies this morning from Judd Street. But I don't think we left you any.'

With these words the affair begins at last.

A toneless voice, that comes as though from the wings of a theatre, in a doomed production of a terrible play, says from the head of the stairs, 'No, I put aside a cup for him. He was the one who told us about that place. Remember?'

He descends as he speaks. Hard to believe that this too-well-timed entrance, these clumsy, improbable lines were rehearsed in the small hours by drunks.

The styrofoam container with its plastic lid and straw is in the fridge, which opens and closes now. Claude sets it down before my father with a breathy, maternal, 'There.'

'Thanks. But I'm not sure I can face it.'

An early mistake. Why let the contemptible brother rather than the sensuous wife bring the man his drink? They'll need to keep him talking and then let's hope he'll change his mind. *Let's*? This is how it is, how stories

94

work, when we know of murders from their inception. We can't help siding with the perpetrators and their schemes, we wave from the quayside as their little ship of bad intent departs. Bon voyage! It's not easy, it's an achievement, to kill someone and go free. The datum of success is 'the perfect murder'. And perfection is hardly human. On board, things will go wrong, someone will trip on an uncoiled rope, the vessel will drift too far west of south. Hard work, and all at sea.

Claude takes a seat at the table, draws a busy breath, plays his best card. Small talk. Or what he considers small talk to be.

'These migrants, eh? What a business. And don't they envy us from Calais! The Jungle! Thank God for the English Channel.'

My father can't resist. 'Ah, England, bound in with the triumphant sea, whose rocky shore beats back the envious siege.'

These words raise his mood. I think I hear him draw the cup towards him. Then he says, 'But I say, invite 'em all in. Come on! An Afghan restaurant in St John's Wood.'

'And a mosque,' says Claude. 'Or three. And wife-beaters and girl-abusers by the thousand.'

'Did I ever tell you about the Goharshad mosque in Iran? I saw it once at dawn. Stood there amazed. In tears. You can't imagine the colours, Claude. Cobalt, turquoise, aubergine, saffron, the palest green, crystal white and everything in between.'

I've rarely heard him call his brother by his name. A strange elation has seized my father. Showing off to my mother, letting her know by comparison what she'll be missing.

Or freeing himself from the clammy musings of his brother, who now says in a tone of cautious compromise, 'Never considered Iran. But Sharm el-Sheikh, the Plaza hotel. Lovely. All the trimmings. Almost too hot for the beach.'

'I'm with John,' my mother says. 'Syrians, Eritreans, Iraqis. Even Macedonians. We need their youth. And darling, will you bring me a glass of water.'

Claude is instantly at the kitchen sink. From there he says, 'Need? I don't *need* to be hacked to pieces in the street. Like Woolwich.' He comes back to the table with two glasses. One is for himself. I think I see where this is heading.

He continues, 'Haven't been down the Tube since seven-seven.'

In the voice he uses to talk past Claude, my father says, 'I saw it calculated once. If sex between the races goes on as now, in five thousand years everyone on earth will be the same pale coffee colour.'

'I'll drink to that,' my mother says.

'I'm not against it really,' Claude says. 'So cheers.'

'To the end of race,' my father agreeably proposes. But I don't think he's raised his cup. Instead, he turns to the matters in hand. 'If you don't mind, I'll pop round with Elodie on Friday. She wants to measure up for curtains.'

I picture a hayloft, off which a hundred-kilo sack of grain is tossed to the granary floor. Then another, and a third. Such are the thuds of my mother's heart.

'That's fine, of course,' she says in a reasonable voice. 'We could give you lunch.'

'Thanks, but we've a crowded day. And now I should be going. The traffic's heavy.'

The scrape of a chair – and how loud, despite the greasy tiles, they sound down here, like the bark of a dog. John Cairncross rises to his feet. He assumes again a friendly tone. 'Trudy, it's been—'

But she's standing too and thinking fast. I feel it in her sinews, in the stiffening drapes of her omentum. She has one last throw and everything rests on an easiness of manner. She cuts him off in a rush of sincerity. 'John, before you go I want to tell you this. I know I can be difficult, sometimes even a bitch. More than half the blame for all this is mine. I know that. And I'm sorry the house is a tip. But what you said last night. About Dubrovnik.'

'Ah,' my father affirms. 'Dubrovnik.' But he's already several feet away.

'What you said was right. You brought it all back to me and it pierced my heart. It was a masterpiece, John, what we created. What's happened since doesn't lessen it. You were so wise to say that. It was beautiful. Nothing that happens in the future can wash it away. And even though it's only water in my glass, I want to raise it to you, to us, and thank you for reminding me. It doesn't matter whether love endures. What matters is that it exists. So. To love. Our love. As it was. And to Elodie.'

Trudy lifts the glass to her lips. The rise and fall of her epiglottis, and her snaky peristalsis briefly deafen me. In all the time I've known her, I've never heard my mother make a speech. Not her way. But curiously evocative. Of what? A nervous schoolgirl, the new head girl making an impression with defiant tremor, emphatic platitudes, before headmaster, staff and the whole school.

A toast to love and therefore death, to Eros and Thanatos. It appears to be a given of intellectual life, that when two notions are sufficiently far apart or opposed, they are said to be profoundly linked. Since death is opposed to everything in life, various couplings are proposed. Art and death. Nature and death. Worryingly, birth and death. And joyously iterated, love and death. On this last and from where I am, no two notions could be more mutually irrelevant. The dead love no one, nothing. As soon as I'm out and about I might try my hand at a monograph. The world cries out for fresh-faced empiricists.

When my father speaks, he sounds closer. He's coming back to the table.

'Well,' he says, most genially, 'that's the spirit.'

I swear the deathly, loving cup is in his hand.

Again, with both heels I kick and kick against his fate.

'Oh, oh, little mole,' my mother calls out in a sweet, maternal voice. 'He's waking up.'

'You failed to mention my brother,' John Cairncross says. It's in his manly poet's nature to amplify another's toast. 'To our future loves, Claude and Elodie.'

'To us all then,' says Claude.

A silence. My mother's glass is already empty.

Then comes my father's drawn-out sigh of satisfaction. Exaggerated to a degree, merely out of politeness. 'More sugary than usual. But not bad at all.'

The styrofoam cup he sets upon the table makes a hollow sound.

It comes back to me, as bright as a cartoon light bulb. A programme on pet care laid out the dangers while Trudy was brushing her teeth one rainy morning after breakfast: unlucky the dog that licks the sweet green liquid off a garage floor. Dead within hours. Just as Claude told it. Chemistry without mercy, purpose or regrets. My mother's electric toothbrush drowned out the rest. We're bound by the same rules that dog our pets. The great chain of non-being is round our necks too.

'Well,' my father says, meaning more than he can know, 'I'll be going.'

Claude and Trudy stand. This is the reckless thrill of the poisoner's art. The substance ingested, the act not yet complete. Within two miles of here are many hospitals, many stomach pumps. But the line of criminality has been crossed. No calling in the deed. They can only stand back and wait for the antithesis, for the antifreeze to leave him cold.

Claude says, 'Is this your hat?'

'Oh yes! I'll take that.'

Is this the last time I hear my father's voice?

We're moving towards the stairs, then up them, the poet leading the way. I have lungs but no air to shout a warning or weep with shame at my impotence. I'm still a creature of the sea, not a human like the others. Now we're passing through the shambles of the hall. The front door is opening. My father turns to give my mother a peck upon the cheek and throw an affectionate punch at his brother's shoulder. Perhaps for the first time in his life.

As he goes out he calls over his shoulder, 'Let's hope that bloody car starts.'

ELEVEN

A PALE, THIN PLANT SEEDED by drunks in the small hours struggles for the remote sunlight of success. Here's the plan. A man is found lifeless at his steering wheel. On the floor of his car by the rear seat, almost out of sight, is a styrofoam cup bearing the logo of a business in Judd Street, near Camden Town Hall. In the cup, the remains of a pureed fruit drink, laced with glycol. Near the cup, an empty bottle of the same lethal substance. Near the bottle, a discarded receipt for the drink bearing that day's date. Concealed under the driver's seat, a few bank statements, some for a small publishing house, others for a personal account. Both show overdrafts in the low tens of thousands. On one of the statements is scrawled, in the handwriting of the deceased, the word 'Enough!' (Trudy's 'thing'.) By the bank statements, a pair of gloves the dead man wore now and then to conceal his psoriasis. They partly conceal a balled-up newspaper page bearing a hostile review of a recent volume of poems. On the front passenger seat, a black hat.

The Metropolitan Police are understaffed, overstretched. The younger detectives, so the older complain, investigate at their screens, reluctant to waste shoe leather. When there are other, gory cases to pursue, a conclusion in this is conveniently at hand. The means unusual but not rare, easily available, palatable, fatal in large doses, and a well-known resource for crime writers. Enquiries suggest that as well as debts, the marriage was in trouble, the wife now living with the brother of the dead man, who had been depressed for months. Psoriasis undermined his confidence. The gloves he wore to conceal it explains the absence of fingerprints on the cup and the antifreeze bottle. CCTV images show him at Smoothie Heaven wearing his hat. He was on his way to the home in St John's Wood that morning. Apparently, he couldn't face becoming a father, or the collapse of his business or his failure as a poet, or his loneliness in Shoreditch, where he was living in rented accommodation. After a row with his wife he left in distress. The wife blames herself. The interview with her had to be suspended a few times. The brother of the dead man was also present and did his best to be helpful.

Is reality so easily, so minutely arranged in advance? My mother, Claude and I are waiting tensely at the open front door. Between the conception of a deed and its acting out lies a tangle of hideous contingencies. At the first touch, the engine turns but does not start. No surprise. This vehicle belongs to a dreaming sonneteer. On the second attempt, the same wheezing failure, and so too on the third. The starter motor is sounding like an old man grown too feeble to clear his throat. If John Cairncross dies on our hands, we'll all go down. Likewise if he survives on our hands. He pauses before trying again, gathering his luck. The fourth is weaker than the third. I conjure a view of him through the car's wind-screen, mimicking for us a quizzical shrug, his form almost obliterated by reflections of summer clouds.

'Oh dear,' says Claude, a man of the world. 'He's going to flood the carb.'

My mother's viscera orchestrate her desperate hopes. But on the fifth, a transformation. With slow heaving and comical popping sounds, the engine internally combusts. Trudy and Claude's straggling plant grows a hopeful bud. As the car reverses into the road my mother has a fit of coughing from what I take to be a cloud of blue exhaust blowing our way. We come inside, and the door is slammed shut.

We're not returning to the kitchen, but climbing the stairs. Nothing is said, but the quality of silence — creamily thick — suggests that more than fatigue and drink are drawing us towards the bedroom. Misery on misery. This is savage injustice.

Five minutes later. This is the bedroom and it's already started. Claude crouches by my mother and might already be naked. I hear his breath on her neck. He's undressing her, to date a peak of sensual generosity unscaled by him.

'Careful,' Trudy says. 'Those buttons are pearls.'

He grunts in reply. His fingers are inexpert, working solely for his own needs. Something of his or hers lands on the bedroom floor. A shoe, or trousers with heavy belt. She's writhing strangely. Impatience. He issues a command in the form of a second grunt. I'm cowering. This is ugly, sure to go wrong, too late in my term. I've been saying this for weeks. I'll suffer.

Obediently, Trudy's on all fours. It's *a posteriori*, doggy style, but not for my sake. Like a mating toad, he clasps himself against her back. On her, now in her, and deep. So little of my treacherous mother separates me from the would-be murderer of my father. Nothing is the same this Saturday noon in St John's Wood. This is not the usual brief and frantic encounter that might threaten the integrity of a brand-new skull. Rather, a glutinous drowning, like something pedantic crawling through a swamp. Mucous membranes slide past each other with a faint creak on the turn. Hours of scheming have accidentally delivered the conspirators into the art of deliberative lovemaking. But nothing passes between them. Mechanically they churn in slow motion, a blind industrial process at half power. All they want is release, to clock out, taste a few seconds' respite from themselves. When it comes, in close succession, my mother gasps in horror. At what she must return to, and might yet see. Her lover emits his third grunt of the shift. They fall apart to lie on their backs on the sheets. Then we all sleep.

On and on through the afternoon, and it's on this long flat stretch of time that I have my first dream, in full colour and rich visual depth. The line, the stated border, between dreaming and waking is vague. No fences or fire break in the trees. Only vacant sentry huts mark the crossing. I begin indistinctly in this new land, as a tyro must, with a formless mass or mess of wavering, ill-lit shapes, people and places dissolving, indistinct voices in vaulted spaces singing or speaking. As I pass through, I feel the pain of unnamed, unreachable remorse, a sense of having left someone or something behind in a betrayal of duty or love. Then it comes beautifully clear. A cold mist on the day of my desertion, a three-day journey on horseback, long rows of the sullen English poor in the rutted lanes, giant elms looming over flooded meadows by the Thames, and at last the familiar thrill and din of the city. In the streets the odour of human waste as solid as house walls, yielding around a narrow corner to the aroma of roasted meat and rosemary and a drab entranceway I pass through to see a young man of my age in the dark-beamed gloom at a table pouring wine from an earthenware jug, a handsome man, leaning in across a smeared oak table, holding me with a tale he has in mind, something he has written or I have, and wants an opinion, or to give one, a correction, a point of fact. Or he wants me to tell him how to go on. This blurring of identity is one aspect of the love I feel for him, which almost smothers the guilt I want to leave behind. Outside in the street a bell tolls. We crowd outside to wait for the funeral cortège. We know this is an important death. The procession doesn't appear, but the bell keeps ringing.

* * *

It's my mother who hears the doorbell. Before I've drifted upwards from the novelty of dream-logic, she's in her dressing gown and we're descending the stairs. As we reach the last run, she gives a cry of surprise. I would guess the midden has been cleared while we slept. The bell sounds again, loud, hard, angry. Trudy is opening the door as she shouts, 'For God's sake! Are you drunk? I'm going as fast as—'

She falters. If she has faith in herself she shouldn't be astonished to see what dread has already let me see: a policeman, no, two, removing their hats.

A kind, fatherly voice says, 'Are you Mrs Cairncross, wife of John?'

She nods.

'Sergeant Crowley. I'm afraid we have some very bad news. May we come in?'

'Oh God,' my mother remembers to say.

They follow us into the sitting room, rarely used and almost clean. If the hallway hadn't been cleared, I think my mother would have been an immediate suspect. Police work is intuitive. What remains, possibly, is a lingering smell, easily confused with exotic cooking.

A second voice, younger, with brotherly solicitude, says, 'We'd like you to be sitting down.'

The sergeant breaks the news. Mr Cairncross's car was reported on the hard shoulder of the M1 northbound, twenty miles from London. His door was open, and not far off, on a grassy embankment, he lay face down. An ambulance came, resuscitation was attempted during the race to hospital, but he died along the way.

A sob, like an air bubble in deep water, rises through my mother's body, rises through me, to burst into the faces of the attentive police.

'Oh God!' she shouts. 'We had the most awful row this morning.' She hunches forward. I feel her put her hands to her face and start to shiver.

'I should tell you this,' the same policeman continues. He pauses delicately, mindful of the double respect owed to the heavily pregnant bereaved. 'We tried to contact you this afternoon. A friend of his identified the body. I'm afraid our first impression is suicide.'

When my mother straightens her spine and lets out

a cry, I'm overcome by love for her, for all that's lost – Dubrovnik, poetry, daily life. She loved him once, as he her. Summoning this fact, erasing others, lifts her performance.

'I should have . . . I should have kept him here. Oh my God, it's all my fault.'

How clever, hiding in plain sight, behind the truth.

The sergeant says, 'People often say that. But you mustn't, you shouldn't. It's wrong to go blaming yourself.'

A deep inhalation and sigh. She seems about to speak, stops, sighs again, gathers herself. 'I ought to explain. Things weren't going well between us. He was seeing someone, he moved out. And I started a . . . His brother moved in with me. John took it badly. That's why I'm saying . . .'

She's got in first with Claude, told them what they were bound to discover. If, in flagrant mood, she were to say now, 'I killed him,' she'd be safe.

I hear the rasp of Velcro, the flip of notebook page, the scratch of pencil. She tells them in dulled voice all that she'd rehearsed, returning at the end to her own culpability. She should never have let him drive away in such a state.

The younger man says reverentially, 'Mrs Cairncross. You weren't to know.'

Then she changes tack, almost sounds cross. 'I don't think I'm taking this in. I'm not even sure I believe you.'

'That's understandable.' This is the paternal sergeant. With polite coughs, he and his colleague stand, ready to leave. 'Is there someone you can call? Someone who can be with you?'

My mother considers her reply. She's bent over again, face in hands. She speaks through her fingers in a flat voice. 'My brother-in-law's here now. He's upstairs asleep.'

The guardians of the rule of law might be exchanging a lewd glance. Any token of their scepticism would help me.

'When the time's right we'd like a word with him as well,' the younger one says.

'This news is going to kill him.'

'I expect you'd like to be alone together now.'

There it is again, the slender lifeline of insinuation to support my cowardly hope that the Force – Leviathan, not I – will take revenge.

I need a moment alone, beyond the reach of voices. I've been too absorbed, too impressed by Trudy's art to peer into the pit of my own grief. And beyond it, the mystery of how love for my mother swells in proportion to my hatred. She's made herself my only parent. I won't survive without her, without the enveloping green gaze to smile into, the loving voice pouring sweets in my ear, the cool hands tending my private parts.

The constabulary leave. My mother mounts the stairs

with a plodding tread. Hand firmly on the banister. One-two and pause, one-two and pause. She's making a repeated humming sound on a fading note, a moan of pity or sadness exhaled through her nostrils. *Nnng . . . nnng*. I know her. Something's building, a prelude to a reckoning. She devised a plot, pure artifice, a malign fairy tale. Now her fanciful story is deserting her, crossing the border as I did this afternoon, but in reverse, past the watchless guard huts, to rise against her, and side with the socially real, the dull quotidian of the working-day world, of human contacts, appointments, obligations, video cameras, computers with inhuman memories. In short, consequences. The tale has turned tail.

Hammered by drink and lost sleep, bearing me upwards, she continues towards the bedroom. *It was never meant to work*, she's telling herself. *It was just my foolish spite. I'm only guilty of a mistake.*

The next step is close, but she won't take it yet.

TWELVE

WE ARE ADVANCING ON slumbering Claude, a hump, a bell-curve of sound baffled by bedclothes. On the exhalation, a long, constipated groan, its approaching terminus frilled with electric sibilants. Then an extended pause which, if you loved him, might alarm you. Has he breathed his last? If you don't, there's hope he has. But finally, a shorter, greedy intake, scarred with the rattle of wind-dried mucus and, at the breezy summit, the soft palate's triumphant purr. The rising volume announces we are very close. Trudy says his name. I feel her hand extend towards him while he's on a downward plunge through the sibilants. She's impatient, she needs to share their success and her touch on his shoulder isn't gentle. He coughs into half-life, like his brother's car, and takes some seconds to find the words to pose his question.

'What the fuck?'

'He's dead.'

'Who?'

'Jesus! Wake up.'

Drawn from the deepest phase of sleep, he has to sit on the edge of the bed, so the complaining mattress says, and wait for his neural circuitry to restore him to the story of his life. I'm young enough not to take such wiring for granted. So, where was he? Ah, yes, attempting to murder his brother. Truly dead? Finally, he's Claude again.

'Well blow me down!'

Now he feels like getting up. It's 6 p.m., he notes. Enlivened, he stands, stretches his arms athletically with a creak of bone and gristle, then moves between bedroom and bathroom cheerily whistling, with full vibrato. From the light music I've heard I know this to be the theme tune from *Exodus*. Grandiose, in a corrupted romantic style, to my newly formed ear, redemptive orchestral poetry to Claude's. He's happy. Meanwhile, Trudy sits in silence on the bed. It's brewing. At last, in dulled monotone she tells him of the visit, the kindness of the police, the discovery of the body, the early presumption as to cause of death. To each of these, delivered as bad news, Claude chimes, 'Marvellous.' He leans forward with a moan to tie his laces.

She says, 'What did you do with the hat?'

She means my father's fedora with the broad brim.

'Didn't you see? I gave it to him.'

'What did he do with it?'

'He had it in his hand when he left. Don't worry. You're *worried*.'

She sighs, thinks for a while. 'The police were so nice.'

'Bereaved wife and all.'

'I don't trust them.'

'Just sit tight.'

'They'll be back.'

'Sit . . . tight.'

He delivers these two words with emphasis and a sinister break between them. Sinister, or fractious.

Now he's in the bathroom again, brushing his hair, no longer whistling. The air is changing.

Trudy says, 'They want to talk to you.'

'Of course. His brother.'

'I told them about us.'

There's a silence before he says, 'Bit dumb.'

Trudy clears her throat. Her tongue is dry. 'No it isn't.'

'Let them find out. Or they'll think you're hiding something, trying to stay one step ahead.'

'I told them John was depressed about us. One more reason for him to—'

'OK, OK. Not bad. Might even be true. But.' He trails away, uncertain of what it is he thinks she should know.

That John Cairncross might have killed himself for love of her, if she hadn't killed him first – there's both pathos and guilt in this recursive notion. I think she doesn't like Claude's casual, even dismissive tone. Just my guess. However close you get to others, you can never get inside them, even when you're inside them. I think she's feeling wounded. But she says nothing yet. We both know it will come soon.

The old question arises. How stupid is Claude really? From the bathroom mirror he follows her thinking. He knows how to counter sentimentality in the matter of John Cairncross. He calls out, 'They'll be wanting to talk to that poet.'

Summoning her is a balm. Every cell in Trudy's body concedes the death her husband owed. She hates Elodie more than she loves John. Elodie will be suffering. Blood-born well-being sweeps through me and I'm instantly high, thrown forwards by a surfer's perfect breaking wave of forgiveness and love. A tall, sloping, smoothly tubular wave that could carry me to where I might start to think fondly of Claude. But I resist it. How diminishing, to accept at second hand my mother's every rush of feeling and be bound tighter to her crime. But it's hard to be separate from her when I need her. And with such churning of emotion, need translates to love, like milk to butter.

She says in a sweet, reflective voice, 'Oh yes, they'll need to talk to Elodie.' Then she adds, 'Claude, you know I love you.'

But he doesn't take this in. He's heard it too often. Instead he says, 'Wouldn't mind being the proverbial fly on the wall.'

Oh proverbial fly, oh wall, when will he learn to speak without torturing me? Speaking's just a form of thinking and he must be as stupid as he appears.

Emerging from the bathroom's echo with a change of subject, he says lightly, 'I might have found us a buyer. A long shot. But I'll tell you later. Did the police leave their cards? I'd like to see their names.'

She can't remember and nor can I. Her mood is shifting again. I think she's staring at him fixedly as she says simply, 'He's *dead*.'

It is indeed a startling fact, barely believable, momentous, like a world war just declared, the prime minister speaking to the nation, families huddled together and the lights gone dim for reasons the authorities won't disclose.

Claude is standing close by her, his hand is on her thigh as he draws her to him. They kiss at length, in deep with their tongues and tangled breath.

'As a doornail,' he murmurs into her mouth. His erection is hard against my back. Then, whispering, 'We did it. Together. We're brilliant together.'

'Yes,' she says between the kisses. It's hard to hear for the rustling of clothes. Her enthusiasm may not be equal to his.

'I love you, Trudy.'

'And I love you.'

Something uncommitted about this 'and'. When she

advanced, he retreated, now the reverse. This is their dance.

'Touch me.' Not quite a command, for his pleading voice is small. She tugs on the zip. Crime and sex, sex and guilt. More dualities. The sinuous movement of her fingers is conveying pleasure. But not enough. He's pressing on her shoulders, she's going down on her knees, lowering herself, taking 'him', as I've heard them say, into her mouth. I can't imagine wanting such a thing for myself. But it's a lifted burden to have Claude satisfied many kindly inches away. It bothers me that what she swallows will find its way to me as nutrient, and make me just a little like him. Why else did cannibals avoid eating morons?

It's over quickly, with barely a gasp. He steps back and secures his zip. My mother swallows twice. He's offering nothing in return and I think she doesn't want it. She steps past him, crosses the bedroom to the window and stands there, her back to the bed. I think of her gazing out towards the tower blocks. My unhappy dream of a future there is nearer now. She repeats quietly, more to herself, for he's splashing once more in the bathroom, 'He's dead . . . dead.' She doesn't seem convinced. And after several seconds, in a murmur, 'Oh God.' Her legs are shaking. She's about to cry, but no, this is too serious for tears. She has yet to comprehend her own news. The twinned facts are huge and she stands too close to see entirely the double horror: his death, and her part in it.

I hate her and her remorse. How did she step from John to Claude, from poetry to dribbling cliché? Step down to the nasty sty to roll in filth with her idiot-lover, lie in shit and ecstasy, plan a house-theft, inflict monstrous pain and a humiliating death on a kindly man. And now gasp and shiver at what she did, as if the murderess were someone else – some sad sister fled from the locked ward with poison on the brain, and out of control, an ugly, chain-smoking sister with sinister compulsions, the long-time family shame, to be sighed for with 'Oh God' and reverent whispering of my father's name. There she goes, in seamless transit, on the very same day and without a blush, from slaughter to self-pity.

Claude appears behind her. The hands on her shoulders again are those of a man newly freed by orgasm, a man eager for practicalities and worldly speculation not compatible with a mind-fogging erection.

'You know what? I was reading the other day. And I've just realised. It's what we should have used. Diphenhydramine. Kind of antihistamine. People are saying the Russians used it on that spy they locked in a sports bag. Poured it into his ear. Turned up the radiators before they left so the chemical dissolved in his tissues without a trace. Dumped the bag in the bath, didn't want fluids dripping on the neighbours in the flat below—'

'That's enough.' She doesn't say it sharply. More in resignation.

'Dead right. Enough's enough. We got there anyway.' He croons a snatch. 'They said you're screwed, your act's too crude, but we came throuuugh.' The bedroom floorboards yield under my mother's feet. He's doing a little dance.

She doesn't turn but stands very still. She's hating him as much as I just hated her. Now he's at her side, sharing the view, trying to find her hand.

'Point is this,' he says importantly. 'They'll interview us separately. We should be lining up our stories. So. He came round this morning. For coffee. Very depressed.'

'I said we had a row.'

'OK. When?'

'Just as he was leaving.'

'What about?'

'He wanted me to move out.'

'Good. So. He came round this morning. For coffee. Very depressed and—'

She sighs, as I would. 'Look. Tell everything as it was, minus the smoothies, plus the row. It doesn't need a rehearsal.'

'OK. This evening. This evening, I'll do the cups, the lot. Across three locations. Another thing. He was wearing gloves the whole time.'

'I know.'

'And when you do the kitchen, not an atom of smoothie to—'

'I *know*.'

He leaves her side to take a turn, a shuffle about the room. He senses success, he's restless, itchy, excited. That she isn't too boosts his impatience. There are things to do, and if not, things to plan. He wants to be out there. But where? He's half humming, half singing something new. 'Baby, baby I love you . . .' I'm not reassured. He's back by us, and she's rigid by the window, but he doesn't sense the danger.

'On the sale,' he says, breaking off his song. 'In my heart of hearts, I always thought we might need to take less than market price just in case we have to make a quick—'

'Claude.'

She mutters his name on two notes, the second lower than the first. A warning.

But he pushes on. I've never known him happier, or less likeable. 'This guy's a builder, a developer. Doesn't even need to look around. Square footage is all. Flats, see. And *cash* in—'

She turns. 'Are you not even aware?'

'Of what?'

'Are you really so incredibly stupid?'

The very question. But Claude has switched moods too. He can sound dangerous.

'Let's hear it.'

'It's escaped your attention.'

'Clearly.'

'Today, just a few hours ago.'

'Yes?'

'I lost my husband—'

'No!'

'The man I once loved, and who loved me, and who shaped my life, gave meaning to it . . .' A clenching in the sinews of her throat prevents her saying more.

But Claude is launched. 'My darling little mouse, that's terrible. Lost, you say. Where could you have put him? Where did you have him last? You must have put him down somewhere.'

'Stop it!'

'Lost! Let me think now. I know what! I've just remembered. You left him on the M1, by the edge of the road, lying on the grass with a gut full of poison. Fancy us forgetting that.'

He might have gone on but Trudy swings back her arm and hits him in the face. Not a lady's slap, but a clenched-fist blow that levers my head from its mooring.

'You're full of spite,' she says with surprising calm. 'Because you were always jealous.'

'Well, well,' says Claude, his voice only a little thickened. 'The naked truth.'

'You hated your brother because you could never be the man he was.'

'While you loved him to the end.' Claude has reverted to fake wonderment. 'Now what was that awfully clever thing someone was saying to me, was it last night or the night before? "I want him dead and it has to be tomorrow." Not the loving wife of my brother, who shaped her life.'

'You got me drunk. That's what you mostly do.'

'And next morning who was that, proposing a toast to love, coaxing the man who shaped her life to raise a cup of venom? Surely not my brother's loving wife. Oh no, not my own darling mouse.'

I understand my mother, I know her heart. She's dealing with the facts as she sees them. The crime, once a sequence of plans and their enactment, now in memory resembles an object, unmoveable, accusing, a cold stone statue in a clearing in a wood. A midwinter's bitter midnight, a waning moon, and Trudy is hurrying away down a frosty woodland path. She turns to look back at the distant figure, partly obscured by bare boughs and skeins of mist, and she sees that the crime, the object of her thoughts, is not a crime at all. It's a mistake. It always was. She suspected it all along. The further she removes herself, the clearer it becomes. She was merely wrong, not bad, and she's no criminal. The crime must be else-where in the woods, and belong to someone else. No arguing with the facts that lead to Claude's essential guilt. His sneering tone can't protect him. It condemns him.

And yet. And yet. And yet she violently wants him. Whenever he calls her his mouse, a curlicue of thrill, a cold contraction lodges in her perineum, an icy hook that tugs her downwards onto a narrow ledge and reminds her of the chasms she's swooned into before, the Walls of Death she's survived too often. His mouse! What humiliation. In the palm of his hand. Pet. Powerless. Fearful. Contemptible. Disposable. Oh to be his mouse! When she knows it's madness. So hard to resist. Can she fight it?

Is she a woman or a mouse?

THIRTEEN

A SILENCE I CAN'T READ follows Claude's mockery. He may regret his sarcasm or resent being diverted from his breezy upland of elation. She may be resentful too, or wanting to resume as his mouse. I'm weighing these possibilities as he moves away from her. He sits on the end of the disordered bed, tapping on his phone. She remains at the window, her back to the room, facing her portion of London, its diminishing evening traffic, scattered birdsong, lozenges of summer cloud and chaos of roofs.

When at last she speaks her tone is sulky and flat. 'I'm not selling this house just so you can get rich.'

His reply is immediate. It's the same needling voice of derision. 'No, no. We'll be rich together. Or, if you like, poor in separate prisons.'

It's nicely put as a threat. Can she believe him, that he'd take them both down? Negative altruism. Cutting off your nose to spite another's face. What should be her response? I have time to think because she's yet to reply. A little shocked at this implied blackmail, I should say. Logically, she should suggest the same. In theory, they have equal power over each other. Leave this house. Never come back. *Or I'll bring the police down on us both*. But even I know that love doesn't steer by logic, nor is power distributed evenly. Lovers arrive at their first kisses with scars as well as longings. They're not always looking for advantage. Some need shelter, others press only for the hyperreality of ecstasy, for which they'll tell outrageous lies or make irrational sacrifice. But they rarely ask themselves what they need or want. Memories are poor for past failures. Childhoods shine through adult skin, helpfully or not. So do the laws of inheritance that bind a personality. The lovers don't know there's no free will. I haven't heard enough radio drama to know more than that, though pop songs have taught me that they don't feel in December what they felt in May, and that to have a womb may be incomprehensible to those who don't and that the reverse is also true.

Trudy turns to face the room. Her small, faraway voice chills me. 'I'm frightened.'

She already sees how their plans have gone wrong, despite signs of early success. She's shivering. Asserting her innocence isn't viable after all. The prospect of a fight with Claude has shown her how lonely her independence could be. His taste for sarcasm is new to her, it scares her, disorients her. And she wants him, even though his voice, his touch and his kisses are corrupted by what they've done. My father's death won't be confined, it's cut loose from its mortuary slab or stainless-steel drawer and drifted in the evening air, across the North Circular, over those same north London roofs.

It's in the room now, in her hair, on her hands, and on Claude's face – an illuminated mask that gapes without expression at the phone in his hand.

'Listen to this,' he says in a Sunday-breakfast sort of way. 'From a local paper. Tomorrow's. Body of a man seen by hard shoulder of M1 between junctions et cetera and et cetera. Twelve hundred calls from passing motorists to emergency services et cetera. Man pronounced dead on arrival at hospital, confirms police spokeswoman et cetera. Not yet named . . . And here's the thing. "Police are not treating the death as a criminal matter at this stage."'

'At this stage,' she murmurs. Then her voice picks up. 'But you don't understand what I'm trying to—'

'Which is?'

'He's dead. *Dead*! It's so . . . And . . .' Now she's starting to cry. 'And it hurts.'

Claude is merely reasonable. 'What I understand is you wanted him dead and now—'

'Oh John!' she cries.

'So we'll stick our courage to the screwing whatever. And get on with—'

'We've . . . done a . . . terrible thing,' she says, oblivious to the break she's making with innocence.

'Ordinary people wouldn't have the guts to do what we've done. So, here's another one. *Luton Herald and Post*. "Yesterday morning—"'

'Don't! Please don't.'

'All right, all right. Same stuff anyway.'

Now she's indignant. 'They write "dead man" and it's nothing to them. Just words. Typing. They've no idea what it means.'

'But they're right. I happen to know this. Around the world a hundred and five people die every minute. Not far off two a second. Just to give you some perspective.'

Two seconds' pause as she takes this in. Then she begins to laugh, an unwanted, mirthless laugh that turns to sobbing, through which she manages to say at last, 'I hate you.'

He's come close, his hand is on her arm, he murmurs into her ear. 'Hate? Don't get me excited all over again.'

But she has. Through his kisses and her tears she says, 'Please. No. Claude.'

She doesn't turn or push him away. His fingers are below my head, moving slowly.

'Oh no,' she whispers, moving closer to him. 'Oh no.'

Grief and sex? I can only theorise. Defences weak, soft tissues gone softer, emotional resilience yielding to childish trust in salty abandonment. I hope never to find out.

He has pulled her towards the bed, removed her sandals, her cotton summer dress and called her his mouse again, though only once. He pushes her onto her back. Consent has rough edges. Does a grieving woman grant it when she raises her buttocks so her panties are pulled free? I'd say no. She has rolled onto her side – the only initiative she takes. Meanwhile, I'm working on a plan, a gesture of last resort. My last shot.

He's kneeling by her, probably naked. At such a time, what could be worse? He swiftly presents the answer: the high medical risk, at this stage of pregnancy, of the missionary position. With a muttered command – how he charms – he turns her on her back, parts her legs with an indifferent backhand swipe, and gets ready, so the mattress tells me, to lower his bulk onto mine.

My plan? Claude is tunnelling towards me and I must be quick. We're swaying, creaking, under great pressure. A high-pitched electronic sound wails in my ears, my eyes bulge and smart. I need the use of my arms, my hands, but there's so little room. I'll say it fast: I'm going to kill myself. An infant death, a homicide in effect, due to my uncle's reckless assault on a gravid woman well advanced in her third trimester. His arrest, trial, sentence, imprisonment. My father's death half avenged. Half, because murderers don't hang in gentle Britain. I'll give Claude a proper lesson in the art of negative altruism. To take my life I'll need the cord, three turns around my neck of the mortal coil. I hear from far off my mother's sighs. The fiction of my father's suicide will be the in- spiration for my own attempt. Life imitating art. To be stillborn – a tranquil term purged of tragedy – has a simple allure. Now here's the thudding against my skull.

Claude is gaining speed, now at a gallop, hoarsely breathing. My world is shaking, but my noose is in place, both hands are gripping, I'm pulling down hard, back bent, with a bell-ringer's devotion. How easy. A slippery tightening against the common carotid, vital channel beloved of slit-throats. I can do it. Harder! A sensation of giddy toppling, of sound becoming taste, touch becoming sound. A rising blackness, blacker than I've ever seen, and my mother murmuring her farewells.

But of course, to kill the brain is to kill the will to kill the brain. As soon as I start to fade, my fists go limp and life returns. Immediately, I hear signs of robust life – intimate sounds, as through the walls of a cheap hotel. Then louder, louder. It's my mother. There she goes, launched on one of her perilous thrills.

But my own prison wall of death's too high. I've fallen back, into the exercise yard of dumb existence.

Finally, Claude withdraws his revolting weight – I salute his crude brevity – and my space is restored, though I've pins and needles in my legs. Now I'm recovering, while Trudy lies back, limp with exhaustion and all the usual regrets.

* * *

It's not the theme parks of Paradiso and Inferno that I dread most – the heavenly rides, the hellish crowds –

and I could live with the insult of eternal oblivion. I don't even mind not knowing which it will be. What I fear is missing out. Healthy desire or mere greed, I want my life first, my due, my infinitesimal slice of endless time and one reliable chance of a consciousness. I'm owed a handful of decades to try my luck on a freewheeling planet. That's the ride for me – the Wall of Life. I want my *go*. I want to *become*. Put another way, there's a book I want to read, not yet published, not yet written, though a start's been made. I want to read to the end of *My History of the Twenty-First Century*. I want to be there, on the last page, in my early eighties, frail but sprightly, dancing a jig on the evening of December 31st, 2099.

It might end before that date and so it's a thriller of sorts, violent, sensational, highly commercial. A compendium of dreams, with elements of horror. But it's bound to be a love story too, and a heroic tale of brilliant invention. For a taste, look at the prequel, the hundred years before. A grim read, at least until halfway, but compelling. A few redeeming chapters on, say, Einstein and Stravinsky. In the new book, one of many unresolved plot lines is this: will its nine billion heroes scrape through without a nuclear exchange? Think of it as a contact sport. Line up the teams. India versus Pakistan, Iran versus Saudi Arabia, Israel versus Iran, USA versus China, Russia versus USA and Nato, North Korea versus the rest. To raise the chances of a score, add more teams: the non-state players will arrive.

How determined are our heroes to overheat their hearth? A cosy 1.6 degrees, the projection or hope of a sceptical few, will open up the tundra to mountains of wheat, Baltic beachside tavernas, lurid butterflies in the Northwest Territories. At the darker end of pessimism, a wind-torn four degrees allows for flood-and-drought calamity and all of turmoil's dark political weather. More narrative tension in subplots of local interest: will the Middle East remain in frenzy, will it empty into Europe and alter it for good? Might Islam dip a feverish extremity in the cooling pond of reformation? Might Israel concede an inch or two of desert to those it displaced? Europa's secular dreams of union may dissolve before the old hatreds, small-scale nationalism, financial disaster, discord. Or she might hold her course. I need to know. Will the USA decline quietly? Unlikely. Will China grow a conscience, will Russia? Will global finance and corporations? Then, bring on the seductive human constants: all of sex and art, wine and science, cathedrals, landscape, the higher pursuit of meaning. Finally, the private ocean of desires – mine, to be bare-foot on a beach round an open fire, grilled fish, juice of lemons, music, the company of friends, someone, not Trudy, to love me. My birthright in a book.

So I'm ashamed of the attempt, relieved to have failed. Claude (now loudly humming in the echoing bathroom) must be reached by other means.

Barely fifteen minutes have passed since he undressed my mother. I sense we're entering a new phase of the evening. Over the sound of running taps he calls out that he's hungry. With the degrading episode behind her and her pulse settling, I believe my mother will be returning to her theme of innocence. To her, Claude's talk of dinner will seem misplaced. Even callous. She sits up, pulls on her dress, finds her knickers in the bedclothes, steps into her sandals and goes to her dressing-table mirror. She begins to braid the hair that, untended, hangs in blonde curls her husband once celebrated in a poem. This gives her time to recover and to think. She'll use the bathroom when Claude has left it. The idea of being near him repels her now.

Disgust restores to her a notion of purity and purpose. Hours ago she was in charge. She could be so again, as long as she resists another sickly, submissive swoon. She's fine for now, she's refreshed, sated, immune, but it waits for her, the little beastie could swell once more into a beast, distort her thoughts, drag her down – and she'll be Claude's. To take charge, however . . . I think of her musing as she tilts her lovely face before the mirror to twist another strand. To give orders as she did this morning in the kitchen, devise the next step, will be to own the offence. If only she could settle down to the blameless grief of the stricken widow.

For now, there are practical tasks. All tainted utensils, plastic cups, the blender itself to be disposed of far from home. The kitchen to be scoured of traces. Only the coffee cups to remain in place on the table, unwashed. These dull chores will keep the horror at a distance for an hour. Perhaps this is why she puts a reassuring hand on the knoll that contains me, near the small of my back. A gesture of loving hope for our future. How could she think of giving me away? She'll need me. I'll brighten the penumbra of innocence and pathos she'll want around her. Mother and child – a great religion has spun its best stories around this potent symbol. Sitting on her knee, pointing skywards, I'll render her immune to prosecution. On the other hand – how I hate that phrase – no preparations have been made for my arrival, no clothes, no furniture, no compulsive nest-making. I've never knowingly been in a shop with my mother. The loving future is a fantasy.

Claude emerges from the bathroom and goes towards the phone. Food is on his mind, an Indian takeaway, so he murmurs. She steps round him and sets about her own ablutions. When we emerge he's still on the phone. He's abandoned Indian for Danish – open sandwiches, pickled herring, baked meats. He's over-ordering, a natural impulse after a murder. By the time he's finished,

Trudy is ready, braided, washed, clean underwear, new frock, shoes in place of sandals, a dab of scent. She's taking charge.

'There's an old canvas bag in the cupboard under the stairs.'

'I'm eating first. I'm starved.'

'Go now. They could be back at any time.'

'I'll do this my way.'

'You'll do as you're—'

Was she really going to say 'told'? What a distance she's travelled, treating him like a child, when just now she was his pet. He might have ignored her. There might have been a row. But what he's doing now is picking up the phone. It's not the Danish people confirming his order, it's not even the same phone. My mother has gone to stand behind him to look. It's not the landline, but the video entryphone. They're staring at the screen, in wonder. The voice comes through, distorted, bereft of lower registers, a thin, penetrating plea.

'Please. I need to see you now!'

'Oh God,' my mother says in plain disgust. 'Not now.'

But Claude, still irritated by being ordered around, has reason to assert his autonomy. He presses the button, replaces the phone, and there's a moment's silence. They have nothing to say to each other. Or too much.

Then we all go downstairs to greet the owl poet.

FOURTEEN

W HILE WE DESCEND THE stairs I have time to
reflect further on my fortunate lack of resolve,
on the self-strangler's self-defeating loop. Some endeav-
ours are doomed at their inception, not by cowardice
but by their very nature. Franz Reichelt, the Flying
Tailor, fatally leapt from the Eiffel Tower in 1912
wearing a baggy parachute suit, certain his invention
could save the lives of aviators. For forty seconds he
paused before the jump. When at last he tilted forward
and stepped into the void, the updraught wrapped the
fabric tightly round his body and he fell just as a stone
would fall. The facts, the mathematics, were against
him. At the foot of the tower he made a shallow grave
in the frozen Parisian ground fifteen centimetres deep.

Which brings me, at Trudy's slow U-turn on the
first landing, via death, to the matter of revenge. It's
coming clearer, and I'm relieved. Revenge: the impulse
is instinctive, powerful – and forgivable. Insulted, duped,
maimed, no one can resist the allure of vengeful
brooding. And here, far out at this extreme, a loved
one murdered, the fantasies are incandescent. We're
social, we once kept each other at bay by violence or its
threat, like dogs in a pack. We're born to this delectable

anticipation. What's an imagination for but to play out and linger on and repeat the bloody possibilities? Revenge may be exacted a hundred times over in one sleepless night. The impulse, the dreaming intention, is human, normal, and we should forgive ourselves.

But the raised hand, the actual violent enactment, is cursed. The maths says so. There'll be no reversion to the status quo ante, no balm, no sweet relief, or none that lasts. Only a second crime. Before you embark on a journey of revenge, dig two graves, Confucius said. Revenge unstitches a civilisation. It's a reversion to constant, visceral fear. Look at the miserable Albanians, chronically cowed by *kanun*, their idiot cult of blood feuds.

So even as we reach the landing outside my precious father's library, I've absolved myself, not of thoughts, but of actions, of avenging his death in this life or in the post-natal next. And I'm absolving myself of cowardice. Claude's elimination won't restore my father. I'm extending Reichelt's forty-second hesitation into a lifetime. No to impetuous action. If I'd succeeded with the cord, then it, not Claude, would have been the cause for any pathologist to note. An unhappy accident, he'd record, and not unusual. There'd be some undeserved relief for my mother and uncle.

If the stairs allow such room for thought it's because Trudy is taking them at the pace of the slowest loris. For once, her hand holds the banister tightly. She takes one step at a time, pauses on some, considers, sighs. I know how things stand. The visitor will hold up the essential housework. The police could return. Trudy's in no mood for a battle of jealous possession. There's an issue of precedence. She's been usurped at the identification of the body – that rankles. Elodie is merely a recent lover. Or not so recent. She might have preceded the move to Shoreditch. Another raw wound to dress. But why call round here? Not to receive or give comfort. She might know or possess some damning tidbit. She could throw Trudy and Claude to the dogs. Or it's blackmail. Funeral arrangements to discuss. None of that. No, no! For my mother, so much effortful negation. How wearying, on top of all else (a hangover, a murder, enervating sex, advanced pregnancy), for my mother to be obliged to exert her will and extend fulsome hatred to a guest.

But she's determined. Her braids tightly conceal her thoughts from all but me, while her underwear – cotton, not silk, I sense – and a short summer print dress, correctly loose but not voluminous, are freshly in place. Her bare, pink arms and legs, her purple-painted toenails, her full, unarguable beauty are on intimidating display. Her aspect is of a ship of the line, fully though reluctantly rigged, gun hatches lowered. A woman-of-war, of which I'm the bow's proud figurehead. She descends in floating but intermittent movements. She'll rise to whatever comes at her.

By the time we reach the hallway it's already started. And badly. The front door has opened and closed. Elodie is in, and in Claude's arms.

'Yes, yes. There, there,' he murmurs into her succession of teary, broken sentences.

'I shouldn't. It's wrong. But I. Oh I'm sorry. What it must be. For you. I can't. Your brother. I can't help it.'

My mother stays at the foot of the stairs, stiffening with distrust, not only of the visitor. So, it's bardic distress.

Elodie is not yet aware of us. Her face must be towards the door. The news she wants to deliver comes in staccato sobs. 'Tomorrow night. Fifty poets. From all over the. Oh, we loved him! Reading in Bethnal. Green library. Or outside. Candles. One poem each. We so want you to be.'

She stops to blow her nose. To do so, she disengages from Claude and sees Trudy.

'Fifty poets,' he helplessly repeats. What notion could be more repugnant to him? 'That's a lot.'

Her sobs are almost under control, but the pathos of her own words brings them on again. 'Oh. Hello Trudy. I'm so, so sorry. If you or. Could say a few. But we'd understand. If you. If you couldn't. How hard it.'

We lose her to her grief, which rises in pitch to a kind of cooing. She tries to apologise and at last we hear, 'Compared to what you. So sorry! Not my place.'

She's right, as Trudy sees it. Usurped again. Out-griefed, out-wailed, she remains, unmoved, by the stairs. Here in the hallway, where the remains of a stench must still linger, we're held in social limbo. We listen to Elodie and the seconds go by. What now? Claude has the answer.

'We'll go down. There's Pouilly-Fumé in the fridge.'

'I don't. I just came to.'

'This way.'

As Claude guides her past my mother, a look must surely pass between them – that is, her flashed rebuke must meet his bland shrug. The two women don't embrace or even touch or speak when they're inches apart. Trudy lets them get ahead before she follows, down into the kitchen, where the two accusers, Glycol and Judd Street Smoothie, hide in forensic smears among the chaos.

'If you'd like,' my mother says as she sets foot on the sticky floorboards, 'I'm sure Claude will make you a sandwich.'

This innocent offer conceals many barbs: it's inappropriate to the occasion; Claude has never made a sandwich in his life; there's no bread in the house; nothing to set between two slabs but the dust of salted nuts. And who could safely eat a sandwich from such a kitchen? Pointedly, she doesn't propose making it herself; pointedly, she casts Elodie and Claude together,

138

distinct from herself. It's an accusation, a rejection, a cold withdrawal bundled into a hospitable gesture. Even as I disapprove, I'm impressed. Such refinements can't be learned from podcasts.

Trudy's hostility has a beneficial effect on Elodie's syntax. 'I couldn't eat a thing, thank you.'

'You could drink a thing,' says Claude.

'I could.'

There follows the familiar suite of sounds – the fridge door, a careless chink of corkscrew against bottle, the cork's sonorous withdrawal, last night's glasses sluiced under the tap. Pouilly. Just across the river from Sancerre. Why not? It's almost seven thirty. The little grapes with their misty grey bloom should suit us well on another hot and airless London evening. But I want more. It seems to me that Trudy and I have not eaten in a week. Stirred by Claude's phone order, I crave as accompaniment an overlooked, old-fashioned dish, *harengs pommes à l'huile*. Slippery smoked herring, waxy new potatoes, the first pressing of the finest olives, onion, chopped parsley – I pine for such an entrée. How elegantly a Pouilly-Fumé would set it off. But how to persuade my mother? I could as easily slit my uncle's throat. The graceful country of my third choice has never seemed so far away.

All of us are at the table now. Claude pours, glasses are raised in sombre tribute to the dead.

Into the silence, Elodie says in an awed whisper, 'But suicide. It just seems so . . . so unlike him.'

'Oh well,' says Trudy, and lets that hang. She's seen an opportunity. 'How long have you known him?'

'Two years. When he taught—'

'Then you wouldn't know about the depressions.'

My mother's quiet voice pushes against my heart. What solace for her, to have faith in a coherent tale of mental illness and suicide.

'My brother wasn't exactly one for the primrose path.'

Claude, I begin to understand, is not a liar of the first rank.

'I didn't know,' Elodie says in a small voice. 'He was always so generous. Especially to us, you know, younger generation who—'

'A whole other side.' Trudy sets this down firmly. 'I'm glad his students never saw it.'

'Even as a child,' says Claude. 'He once took a hammer to our—'

'This isn't the time for that story.' Trudy has made it more interesting by cutting it short.

'You're right,' he says. 'We loved him anyway.'

I feel my mother's hand go up to her face to cover it or brush away a tear. 'But he'd never get treatment. He couldn't accept that he was ill.'

There's protest, or complaint, in Elodie's voice that my mother and uncle won't like. 'It doesn't make any sense. He was on his way to Luton, to pay the printer. In cash. He was so happy to be settling a debt. And he was reading tonight. King's College Poetry Society. Three of us were like, you know, the supporting band.'

'He loved his poems,' Claude says.

Elodie's tone rises with her anguish. 'Why would he pull over and . . . ? Just like that. When he'd finished his book. And been shortlisted for the Auden Prize.'

'Depression's a brute.' Claude surprises me with this insight. 'All the good things in life vanish from your—'

My mother cuts in. Her voice is hard. She's had enough. 'I know you're younger than me. But do I really have to spell it out for you? Company in debt. Personally in debt. Unhappy with his work. Child on the way he didn't want. Wife fucking his brother. Chronic skin complaint. And depression. Is that clear? You think it isn't bad enough without your theatrics, without your poetry readings and prizes and telling *me* it doesn't make sense? You got into his bed. Count yourself lucky.'

Trudy in turn is cut off. By a shriek and the smack of a chair tipping backwards to the floor.

I note at this point that my father has receded. Like a particle in physics, he escapes definition in his flight from us; the assertive, successful poet-teacher-publisher, calmly intent on repossessing his house, his father's house; or the hapless, put-upon cuckold, the unworldly fool cramped by debt and misery and lack of talent. The more we hear of one, the less we believe of the other.

Elodie's first uttered sound is both a word and a sob. 'Never!'

A silence, through which I sense Claude, then my mother, reaching for their drinks.

'I didn't know what he was going to say last night. All untrue! He wanted you back. He was trying to make you jealous. He was never going to throw you out.'

Her voice dips as she bends to right the chair. 'That's why I'm here. To tell you, and you better get this right. Nothing! Nothing happened between us. John Cairncross was my editor and friend and teacher. He helped me become a writer. Is that clear?'

I'm heartlessly suspicious, but they believe her. That she was not my father's lover should be a deliverance for them, but I think it raises other possibilities. An inconvenient woman bearing witness to all the reasons my father had to live. How unfortunate.

'Sit down,' Trudy says quietly. 'I believe you. No more shouting please.'

Claude refills the glasses. The Pouilly-Fumé seems to me too thin, too piercing. Too young, perhaps, not right for the occasion. Summer-evening heat aside, a muscular Pomerol might suit us better when strong emotions are on display. If only there was a cellar, if I could go down there now, into the dusty gloom to pull a bottle off the racks. Stand quietly with it a moment, squint at its label, nod wisely to myself as I bring it up. Adult life, a faraway oasis. Not even a mirage.

I imagine my mother's bare arms folded on the table, eyes steady and clear. No one could guess at her torment. John loved only her. His invocation of Dubrovnik was sincere, his declaration of hatred, his dreams of strangling her, his love for Elodie – all hopeful lies. But she mustn't go down, she must be staunch. She's putting herself in a mode, a mood, of serious probing, seemingly not unfriendly.

'You identified the body.'

Elodie is also calmer. 'They tried to get hold of you. No reply. They had his phone, they saw his calls to me. About the reading tonight – nothing else. I asked my fiancé to go with me, I was so scared.'

'How did he look?'

'She means John,' Claude says.

'I was surprised. He looked peaceful. Except . . .' She draws a sharp, inward sigh. 'Except his mouth. It was so long, so wide, stretched almost ear to ear, like an insane smile. It was closed though. I was glad about that.'

Around me, in the walls and through the crimson chambers that lie beyond them, I feel my mother tremble. One more physical detail like this will undo her.

FIFTEEN

EARLY IN MY CONSCIOUS life one of my fingers, not then subject to my influence, brushed past a shrimp-like protuberance between my legs. And though shrimp and fingertip lay at differing distances from my brain, they felt each other simultaneously, a diverting issue in neuroscience known as the binding problem. Days later it happened again on another finger. Some developmental time passed and I grasped the implications. Biology is destiny, and destiny is digital, and in this case, binary. It was bleakly simple. The strangely essential matter at the heart of every birth was now settled. Either–or. Nothing else. No one exclaims at the moment of one's dazzling coming-out, *It's a person!* Instead: *It's a girl*, *It's a boy*. Pink or blue – a minimal improvement on Henry Ford's offer of cars of any colour so long as they were black. Only two sexes. I was disappointed. If human bodies, minds, fates are so complex, if we are free like no other mammal, why limit the range? I seethed, and then, like everyone else, I settled down and made the best of my inheritance. For sure, complexity would come upon me in time. Until then, my plan was to arrive as a freeborn Englishman, a creature of the post English-as-well-as-Scottish-and-French Enlightenment. My selfhood would be sculpted by pleasure, conflict, experience, ideas and my own judgement, as rocks and trees are shaped by rain, wind and time. Besides, in my confinement I had other concerns: my drink problem, family worries, an uncertain future in which I faced a possible jail sentence or a life in 'care' in the careless lap of Leviathan, fostered up to the thirteenth floor.

But lately, as I track my mother's shifting relation to her crime, I've remembered rumours of a new dispensation in the matter of blue and pink. Be careful what you wish for. Here's a new politics in university life. This digression may seem unimportant, but I intend to apply as soon as I can. Physics, Gaelic, anything. So I'm bound to take an interest. A strange mood has seized the almost-educated young. They're on the march, angry at times, but mostly needful, longing for authority's blessing, its validation of their chosen *identities*. The decline of the West in new guise perhaps. Or the exaltation and liberation of the self. A social-media site famously proposes seventy-one gender options – neutrois, two spirit, bigender . . . any colour you like, Mr Ford. Biology is not destiny after all, and there's cause for celebration. A shrimp is neither limiting nor stable. I declare my undeniable feeling for who I am. If I turn out to be white, I may identify as black. And vice versa. I may announce myself as disabled, or disabled in context. If my identity is that of a believer, I'm easily wounded, my flesh torn to bleeding by any questioning of my faith. Offended, I enter a state of grace. Should inconvenient opinions hover near me like fallen angels or evil djinn (a mile being too near), I'll be in need of the special campus safe room equipped with Play-Doh and looped footage of gambolling puppies. Ah, the intellectual life! I may need advance warning if upsetting books or ideas threaten my very being by coming too close, breathing on my face, my brain, like unwholesome dogs.

I'll feel, therefore I'll be. Let poverty go begging and climate change braise in hell. Social justice can drown in ink. I'll be an activist of the emotions, a loud, campaigning spirit fighting with tears and sighs to shape institutions around my vulnerable self. My identity will be my precious, my only true possession, my access to the only truth. The world must love, nourish and protect it as I do. If my college does not bless me, validate me and give me what I clearly need, I'll press my face into the vice chancellor's lapels and weep. Then demand his resignation.

The womb, or this womb, isn't such a bad place, a little like the grave, 'fine and private' in one of my father's favourite poems. I'll make a version of a womb for my student days, set aside the Enlightenments of Rosbifs, Jocks and Frogs. Away with the real, with dull facts and hated pretence of objectivity. Feeling is queen. Unless she identifies as king.

146

I know. Sarcasm ill suits the unborn. And why digress? Because my mother is in step with new times. She may not know it, but she marches with a movement. Her status as a murderer is a fact, an item in the world outside herself. But that's old thinking. She affirms, she identifies as innocent. Even as she strains to clean up traces in the kitchen, she feels blameless and therefore is – almost. Her grief, her tears, are proof of probity. She's beginning to convince herself with her story of depression and suicide. She can almost believe the sham evidence in the car. Only persuade herself and she'll deceive with ease and consistency. Lies will be *her* truth. But her construction is new and frail. My father's ghastly smile could upend it, that knowing grin coldly stretched across a corpse's face. That's why it's needed, Elodie's validation of my mother's innocent self. And why she leans forward now, taking me with her, listening tenderly to the poet's halting words. For Elodie will soon be in interview with the police. Her beliefs, which will direct her memory and order her account, must be properly shaped.

Claude, unlike Trudy, owns his crime. This is a Renaissance man, a Machiavel, an old-school villain who believes he can get away with murder. The world doesn't come to him through a haze of the subjective; it comes refracted by stupidity and greed, bent as through glass or water, but etched on a screen before the inner eye, a lie as sharp and bright as truth. Claude doesn't know he's stupid. If you're stupid, how can you tell? He may blunder through an undergrowth of clichés, but he understands what he did and why. He'll flourish, without a backward glance, unless caught and punished, and then he'll never blame himself, only his bad luck among random events. He can claim his inheritance, his tenure among the rational. Enemies of the Enlightenment will say he's the embodiment of its spirit. Nonsense!

But I know what they mean.

SIXTEEN

ELODIE ELUDES ME, LIKE a half-remembered song – an unfinished melody indeed. When she squeezed by us in the hall, when she was still, in our thoughts, my father's girl, I listened out for the alluring creak of leather. But no, today she's dressed in softer style, more colourfully, I think. She would have cut a figure at the poetry event tonight. When she was wailing in distress her voice was pure. But her account of the visit to the mortuary, clutching at her fiancé's wrist, was a reminder, as each growling sentence trailed away, of the guttural urbane, her tasty fry-up. Now, as my mother extends an arm across the kitchen table to enfold the visitor's hand in hers, I hear in the vowels the duck's quack restored. Elodie's relaxing into my mother's confidence as she, the poet, praises my father's poems. It's the sonnets she loves most.

'He wrote them in a conversational style, but dense with meaning, and so musical.'

Her use of tense is correct but offensive. She speaks as if the death of John Cairncross has been fully confirmed, absorbed, publicly acknowledged, historically beyond grief like the Sack of Rome. Trudy will mind more than I do. I've been conditioned to believe his poetry was a dud. Today, everything is up for revaluation.

Her voice grave with insincerity, Trudy says, 'It will be a long time before we have the full measure of him as a poet.'

'Oh yes, oh yes! But we already know something. Beyond Hughes. Up there with Fenton, Heaney and Plath.'

'Names to conjure with,' says Claude.

This is my Elodie problem. What is she doing here? She dances like a wild Corybant, in and out of focus. Overpraising my father may be a style of comforting my mother. If so, that's poorly conceived. Or sorrow distorts her judgement. That's forgivable. Or her self-importance is bound up with her patron's. That's not. Or she's come to find out who killed her lover. That's interesting.

Should I like her or distrust her?

My mother loves her and won't let go of her hand. 'You'll know this better than I do. Talent on that scale comes at a cost. Not only to himself. Kind to everyone who isn't close. Strangers too. And people saying, "Almost as kind as Heaney." Not that I ever knew or read him. But just below the surface John was in agony—'

'No!'

'Self-doubt. Constant mental pain. Lashing out at those he loved. But cruellest to himself. Then the poem gets written at last—'

'And then the sun comes out.' Claude has caught his sister-in-law's drift.

She says loudly over him, 'That conversational style? One long bloody battle to wrench it from his soul—'

'Oh!'

'Personal life wrecked. And now—'

She chokes up on the tiny word that contains the fateful present. On such a day of revaluation I could be wrong. But I always thought my father composed fast, with reproachable ease. It was held against him in the review he once read aloud to prove his indifference. I heard him say it to my mother during one of his sad visits: if it doesn't come at once, it shouldn't come. There's a special grace in facility. All art aspires to the condition of Mozart's. Then he laughed at his own presumption. Trudy won't remember. And she'll never know that even as she lied about my father's mental health, his poetry raised her diction. Lashing out? Wrench? Soul? Borrowed clothes!

But they've made an impression. Cold mother, she knows what she's about.

Elodie whispers, 'I never knew.'

Then, another silence. Trudy waits intensely, like an angler whose fly is sweetly placed. Claude starts a word, a mere vowel, severed, I'd guess, by her glance.

Our visitor begins dramatically. 'All John's instructions are engraved on my heart. When to break a line. "Never randomly. Stay at the helm. Make sense, a unit of sense. Decide, decide, decide." And know your scansion so you "disrupt the beat knowingly". Then, "Form isn't a cage. It's an old friend you can only pretend to leave." And feelings. He'd say, "Don't unpack your heart. One detail tells the truth." Also, "Write for the voice, not the page, write for the untidy evening in the parish hall." He made us read James Fenton on the genius of the trochee. Afterwards, he set the assignment for the week ahead – a poem in four stanzas of trochaic tetrameters catalectic. We laughed at this gobbledegook. He had us singing an example, a nursery rhyme. "Boys and girls come out to play." Then he recited from memory Auden's "Autumn Song". "Now the leaves are falling fast, / Nurse's flowers will not last." Why is the missing syllable at the end of the line so effective? We couldn't answer him. Then what about a poem with the weak syllable restored? "Wendy speeded my undressing, / Wendy is the sheet's caressing." He knew the whole of Betjeman's "Indoor Games near Newbury" and made us giggle. So, for that assignment, I wrote the first of my owl poems – in that same metre of "Autumn Song".

'He made us learn our own strongest poems by heart. So we'd be bold at our first reading, stand on stage without our pages. The idea made me nearly faint with fear. Listen, now I'm slipping into trochees!'

Talk of scansion is of interest only to me. I sense my mother's impatience. This has gone on too long. If I had breath to hold, I'd hold it now.

'He bought us drinks, lent us money we never gave back, heard us out on boyfriend–girlfriend trouble, fights with parents, so-called writer's block. He stood bail for one drunken would-be poet in our group. He wrote letters to get us grants, or humble jobs on literary pages. We loved the poets he loved, his opinions became our own. We listened to his radio talks, we went to the readings he sent us to. And we went to his own. We knew his poems, his anecdotes, his catchphrases. We thought we knew him. It never crossed our minds that John, the grown-up, the high priest, had problems too. Or that he doubted his poetry just as we did ours. We mostly worried about sex and money. Nothing like his agony. If only we'd known.'

The fly was taken, the shortening line was taut and trembling, and now the catch is in the keep-net. I feel my mother relax.

That mysterious particle, my father, is gaining mass, growing in seriousness and integrity. I'm caught between pride and guilt.

In a brave, kind voice Trudy says, 'It would have made no difference. You mustn't blame yourself. We knew everything, Claude and I. We tried everything.'

Claude, stirred by the sound of his name, clears his throat. 'Beyond help. His own worst enemy.'

'Before you go,' says Trudy, 'there's a little something I want you to have.'

We climb the stairs to the hall and then to the first floor, my mother and I moving lugubriously, Elodie close behind. The purpose must surely be to let Claude gather up whatever he must dispose of. Now we're standing in the library. I hear the young poet's intake of breath as she looks around at three walls of poetry.

'I'm sorry it smells so musty in here.'

Already. The books, the library air itself, in mourning.

'I'd like you to take one.'

'Oh, I couldn't. Shouldn't you keep it all together?'

'I want you to. So would he.'

And so we wait while she decides.

Elodie is embarrassed and therefore quick. She returns to show her choice.

'John's put his name in it. Peter Porter. *The Cost of Seriousness*. It's got "An Exequy". Tetrameters again. The most beautiful.'

'Ah yes. He came to dinner once. I think.'

On that last word the doorbell sounds. Louder, longer than usual. My mother tenses, her heart begins to pound. What is it she dreads?

'I know you'll have a lot of visitors. Thank you so—'

'Shush!'

We go quietly onto the landing. Trudy leans cautiously over the banisters. Careful now. Distantly we hear Claude talking on the videophone, then his footsteps ascending from the kitchen.

'Oh hell,' my mother whispers.

'Are you all right? Do you need to sit down?'

'I think I do.'

We retreat, the better to be concealed from the front door's line of sight. Elodie helps my mother into the cracked leather armchair in which she used to daydream while her husband recited to her.

We hear the front door open, the murmur of voices, the door closing. Then only one set of footsteps coming back along the hall. Of course, the Danish takeaway, the open sandwiches, my dream of herring about to be fulfilled, in part.

All this Trudy recognises too. 'I'll see you out.'

Downstairs, at the door, just as Elodie is leaving, she turns to say to Trudy, 'I'm due at the police station tomorrow morning, nine o'clock.'

'I'm so sorry. It's going to be hard for you. Just tell them everything you know.'

'I will. Thank you. Thank you for this book.'

They embrace and kiss, and she's gone. My guess is that she's got what she came for.

We return to the kitchen. I'm feeling strange. Famished. Exhausted. Desperate. My worry is that Trudy will tell Claude that she can't face eating. Not after the doorbell. Fear is an emetic. I'll die unborn, a meagre death. But she and I and hunger are one system, and sure enough, the tinfoil boxes are ripped apart. She and Claude eat fast, standing by the kitchen table, where yesterday's coffee cups might still be.

He says through stuffed mouth, 'All packed and ready to go?'

Pickled herring, gherkin, a slice of lemon on pumpernickel bread. They don't take long to reach me. Soon I'm whipped into alertness by a keen essence saltier than blood, by the tang of sea spray off the wide, open ocean road where lonely herring shoals skim northwards through clean black icy water. It keeps coming, a chilling Arctic breeze pouring over my face, as though I stood boldly in the prow of a fearless ship heading into glacial freedom. That is, Trudy eats one open sandwich after another, on and on until she takes a first bite of her last and throws it down. She's reeling, she needs a chair.

She groans. 'That was good! Look, tears. I'm crying with pleasure.'

'I'll be off,' Claude says. 'And you can cry alone.'

For a long time I've been almost too big for this place. Now I'm too big. My limbs are folded hard against my chest, my head is wedged into my only exit. I wear my mother like a tight-fitting cap. My back aches, I'm out of shape, my nails need cutting, I'm beat, lingering in that dusk where torpor doesn't cancel thought but frees it. Hunger, then sleep. One need fulfilled, another takes it place. Ad infinitum, until the needs become mere whims, luxuries. Something in this goes near the heart of our condition. But that's for others. I'm pickled, the herrings are bearing me away, I'm on the shoulders of the giant shoal, heading north, and when I'm there I'll hear the music not of seals and groaning ice, but of vanishing evidence, of running taps, the popping of foaming suds, I'll hear the midnight chime of pots, and chairs upended on the kitchen table to reveal the floor and its scattered burden of food crumbs, human hair and mouse shit. Yes, I was there when he tempted her again to bed, called her his mouse, pinched her nipples hard, filled her cheeks with his lying breath and cliché-bloated tongue.

And I did nothing.

SEVENTEEN

I WAKE INTO NEAR SILENCE to find myself horizontal. As always, I listen carefully. Beyond the patient tread of Trudy's heart, beyond her breathing sighs and faintest creak of ribcage, are the murmurs and trickles of a body maintained by hidden networks of care and regulation, like a well-run city in the dead of night. Beyond the walls, the rhythmic commotion of my uncle's snoring, quieter than usual. Beyond the room, no sound of traffic. In another time I would have turned as best I could and sunk back into dreamlessness. Now, one splinter, one pointed truth from the day before, punctures the delicate tissue of sleep. Then everything, everyone, the small, willing cast, slips in through the tear. Who's first? My smiling father, the new and difficult rumour of his decency and talent. The mother I'm bound to, and bound to love and loathe. Priapic, satanic Claude. Elodie, scanning poet, untrustworthy dactyl. And cowardly me, self-absolved of revenge, of everything but thought. These five figures turn before me, playing their parts in events exactly as they were, and then as they might have been and might yet be. I've no authority to direct the action. I can only watch. Hours pass.

Later, I'm woken by voices. I'm on a slope, which suggests my mother is sitting up in bed propped by pillows. The traffic outside is not yet at its usual density. My guess is 6 a.m. My first concern is that we might be due a matutinal visit to the Wall of Death. But no, they aren't even touching. Conversation only. They've had pleasure enough to last till noon at least, which opens an opportunity now for rancour, or reason, or even regret. They've chosen the first. My mother is speaking in the flat tone she reserves for her resentments. The first complete sentence I understand is this:

'If you weren't in my life, John would be alive today.'

Claude considers. 'Likewise if you weren't in mine.'

A silence follows this blocking move. Trudy tries again. 'You turned silly games into something else, bringing that stuff into the house.'

'The stuff you made him drink.'

'If you hadn't—'

'Listen. Dearest.'

The endearment is mostly menace. He draws breath and considers yet again. He knows he must be kind. But kindness without desire, without promise of erotic reward, is difficult for him. The strain is in his throat. 'It's *fine*. Not a criminal matter. We're on course. That girl's going to say all the right things.'

'Thanks to me.'

'Thanks to you is right. Death certificate, fine. Will,

159

fine. Crem and all the trimmings, fine. Baby and house sale, fine—'

'But four and a half million—'

'Is *fine*. In case of worst case, the plan-B plan – fine.'

Only syntax might make one think that I'm for sale. But I'll be free at the point of delivery. Or worthless.

Trudy repeats with contempt, 'Four and a half million.'

'Fast. No questions.'

A lovers' catechism, which they may have been round before. I'm not always listening. She says, 'Why the hurry?' He says, 'In case things go wrong.' She says, 'Why should I trust you?' He says, 'No choice.'

Have the house-sale papers come already? Has she signed? I don't know. Sometimes I doze and don't hear everything. And I don't care. Having nothing myself, property is not my concern. Skyscrapers, tin shacks, and all the bridges and temples in between. Keep them. My interest is strictly post-partum, the departing hoof mark in the rock, the bleeding lamb drifting skyward. Always up. Hot air without a balloon. Take me with you, chuck the ballast. Give me my *go*, my afterlife, paradise on earth, even a hell, a thirteenth floor. I can take it. I believe in life after birth, though I know that separating hope from fact is hard. Something short of eternity will do. Three score and ten? Wrap them up, I'll take them. On hope – I've been hearing about the latest slaughters in pursuit of dreams of the life beyond. Mayhem in this world, bliss in the next. Fresh-bearded young men with beautiful skin and long guns on Boulevard Voltaire gazing into the beautiful, disbelieving eyes of their own generation. It wasn't hatred that killed the innocents but faith, that famished ghost, still revered, even in the mildest quarters. Long ago, someone pronounced groundless certainty a virtue. Now, the politest people say it is. I've heard their Sunday-morning broadcasts from cathedral precincts. Europe's most virtuous spectres, religion and, when it faltered, godless utopias bursting with scientific proofs, together they scorched the earth from the tenth to the twentieth centuries. Here they come again, risen in the East, pursuing their millennium, teaching toddlers to slit the throats of teddy bears. And here I am with my home-grown faith in the life beyond. I know it's more than a radio programme. The voices I hear are not, or not only, in my head. I believe my time will come. I'm virtuous too.

* * *

The morning is without event. Trudy and Claude's exchange of muted acrimony falters then yields to hours of sleep, after which she leaves him in bed and takes a shower. In the thrumming warmth of speeding droplets and the sound of my mother's tuneful humming, I experience an unaccountable mood of joy and excitement. I can't help myself, I can't hold the happiness back. Are these borrowed hormones? It hardly matters. I see the world as golden, even though the shade is no more than a name. I know it's along the scale near yellow, also just a word. But golden sounds right, I sense it, I taste it where hot water cascades across the back of my skull. I don't remember such carefree delight. I'm ready, I'm coming, the world will catch me, tend to me because it can't resist me. Wine by the glass rather than the placenta, books direct by lamplight, music by Bach, walks along the shore, kissing by moonlight. Everything I've learned so far says all these delights are inexpensive, achievable, ahead of me. Even when the roaring water ceases, when we step into colder air and I'm shaken to a blur by Trudy's towel, I have the impression of singing in my head. Choirs of angels!

Another hot day, another floating confection, so I dream, of printed cotton, yesterday's sandals, no scent because her soap, if it's the bar Claude gave her, is perfumed with gardenia and patchouli. She doesn't braid today. Instead, two plastic devices, highly coloured, I'm sure, attached above her ears hold her hair back on each side. I feel my spirits begin to droop as we descend the familiar stairs. Just now, to have forgotten my father for minutes on end! We enter a clean kitchen, whose unnatural order is my mother's night tribute to him. Her exequy. The acoustic is altered, the floor no longer sticks to her sandals. The flies have moved to other heavens. As she goes towards the coffee machine she must be thinking, as I am, that Elodie will have finished her interview. The officers of the law will be confirming or abandoning their first impressions. In effect, for now, for us, both are true at once. Ahead of us the path seems to fork, but it's forked already. In any event, there will be a visit.

She reaches up to a cupboard for the tin of ground coffee and the filter papers, runs the cold-water tap, fills a jug, fetches a spoon. Most of the cups are clean. She sets out two. There's pathos in this familiar routine, in the sounds of homely objects touching surfaces. And in the little sigh she makes when she turns or slightly bends our unwieldy form. It's already clear to me how much of life is forgotten even as it happens. Most of it. The unregarded present spooling away from us, the soft tumble of unremarkable thoughts, the long-neglected miracle of existence. When she's no longer twenty-eight and pregnant and beautiful, or even free, she won't remember the way she set down the spoon and the sound it made on slate, the frock she wore today, the touch of her sandal's thong between her toes, the summer's warmth, the white noise of the city beyond the house walls, a short burst of birdsong by a closed window. All gone, already.

But today is special. If she forgets the present it's because her heart is in the future, the one that's closing in. She's thinking of the lies she'll have to tell, how they need to cohere, and be consistent with Claude's. This is pressure, this is the feeling she used to have before an exam. A little chill in the gut, some weakness below the knees, a tendency to yawn. She must remember her lines. Cost of failure being higher, more interesting than any routine school test. She could try an old assurance from childhood – *no one will actually die*. That won't do. I feel for her. I love her.

Now I'm feeling protective. I can't quite dispel the worthless notion that the very beautiful should live by other codes. For such a face as I've imagined for her there should be special respect. Prison for her would be an outrage. Against nature. There's already nostalgia in this domestic moment. It's a treasure, a gem for the memory store. I've got her to myself, here in the ordered kitchen, in sunshine and peace, while Claude sleeps away the morning. We should be close, she and I, closer than lovers. There's something we should be whispering to each other.

Perhaps it's goodbye.

EIGHTEEN

In the early afternoon the phone rings and the future introduces herself. Chief Inspector Clare Allison, now attached to the case. The voice sounds friendly, no hint of accusation. That may be a bad sign.

We're in the kitchen again, Claude has the phone. His first coffee of the day is in his other hand. Trudy stands close and we hear both sides. *Case?* The word packs a threat. *Chief* inspector? Also unhelpful.

I gauge my uncle's anxiety by his zeal to accommodate. 'Oh yes. Yes! Of course. Please do.'

Chief Inspector Allison intends to visit us. Normal practice would be for both to come to the station for a chat. Or to make statements, if appropriate. However, due to Trudy's advanced condition, the family's grief, the chief inspector and a sergeant will come by within the hour. She'd like to take a look at the site of the deceased's last contacts.

This last, innocent and reasonable to my ears, puts Claude into a frenzy of welcome. 'Please come. Marvellous. Do. Take us as you find us. Can't wait. You'll—'

She hangs up. He turns towards us, probably ashen, and says in a tone of disappointment, 'Ah.'

Trudy can't resist mimicry. '*All . . . fine*, is it?'

'What's this *case*? It's not a criminal matter.' He appeals to an imaginary audience, a council of elders. A jury.

'I hate it,' my mother murmurs, more to herself. Or to me, I'd like to believe. 'I hate it, I *hate* it.'

'This is supposed to be for the coroner.' Claude walks away from us, aggrieved, takes a turn around the kitchen and comes back to us, outraged. Now his complaint is to Trudy. 'This is *not* a police matter.'

'Oh really?' she says. 'Better phone the inspector and put her straight.'

'That poet woman. I knew we couldn't trust her.'

We understand that somehow Elodie is my mother's charge, that this is an accusation.

'You fancied her.'

'You said she'd be useful.'

'You fancied her.'

But the deadpan reiteration doesn't needle him.

'Who wouldn't? Who cares?'

'I do.'

I ask myself once more what I gain by their falling out. It could bring them down. Then I'll keep Trudy. I've heard her say that in prison nursing mothers have a better life. But I'll lose my birthright, the dream of all humanity, my freedom. Whereas together, as a team, they might scrape through. Then give me away. No mother, but I'll be free. So which? I've been round this before, always returning to the same hallowed place, the only principled decision. I'll risk material comfort and take my chances in the wider world. I've been confined too long. My vote's for liberty. The murderers must escape. This is a good moment then, before the Elodie argument goes too far, for me to give my mother another kick, distract her from squabbling with the interesting fact of my existence. Not once, not twice, but the magic number of all the best old stories. Three times, like Peter's denial of Jesus.

'Oh, oh, oh!' She almost sings it. Claude pulls out a chair for her and brings a glass of water.

'You're sweating.'

'Well I'm hot.'

He tries the windows. They haven't budged in years. He looks in the fridge for ice. The trays are empty in the recent cause of three rounds of gin and tonics. So he sits across from her and extends his cooling sympathies.

'It'll be all right.'

'No, it won't.'

His silence agrees. I was considering a fourth strike, but Trudy's mood is dangerous. She might go on the attack and invite a dangerous response.

After a pause, in mollifying mode, he says, 'We should run through it one last time.'

'What about a lawyer?'

'Bit late now.'

'Tell them we won't talk without one.'

'Won't look good when they're only coming round for a chat.'

'I *hate* this.'

'We should run through it one last time.'

But they don't. Stupefied, they contemplate Chief Inspector Allison's approach. By now, within the hour could mean within the minute. Knowing everything, almost everything, I'm party to the crime, safe, obviously, from questioning, but fearful. And curious, impatient to witness the inspector's skills. An open mind could peel these two apart in minutes. Trudy betrayed by nerves, Claude by stupidity.

I'm trying to place them, the morning coffee cups from my father's visit. Transferred, I now think, to wait unwashed by the kitchen sink. DNA on one cup will prove my mother and uncle to be telling the truth. The Danish debris must be close by.

'Quickly,' says Claude at last. 'Let's do this. Where did the row start?'

'In the kitchen.'

'No. On the doorstep. What was it about?'

'Money.'

'No. Throwing you out. How long was he depressed?'

'Years.'

'Months. How much did I lend him?'

'A thousand.'

'Five. Christ. Trudy.'

'I'm pregnant. It makes you dim.'

'You said it yourself yesterday. Everything as it was, plus the depression, minus the smoothies, plus the row.'

'Plus the gloves. Minus he was moving back in.'

'God yes. Again. What was he depressed about?'

'Us. Debts. Work. Baby.'

'Good.'

They go round a second time. By the third, it sounds better. What sickening complicity that I should wish them success.

'So say it then.'

'As it happened. Minus the smoothies, plus the row and gloves, minus the depression, plus he was moving back in.'

'No. Fuck! Trudy. As was. *Plus* the depression, minus the smoothies, plus the row, plus the gloves, minus he was moving back in.'

The doorbell rings and they freeze.

'Tell them we're not ready.'

This is my mother's idea of a joke. Or evidence of her terror.

Muttering probable obscenities, Claude goes towards the videophone, changes his mind and makes for the stairs and the front door.

Trudy and I take a nervous shuffle around the kitchen. She too is muttering as she works on her story. Usefully, each successive effort of memory removes her further from the actual events. She's memorising her memories. The transcription errors will be in her favour. They'll be a helpful cushion at first, on their way to becoming the truth. She could also tell herself – *she* didn't buy the glycol, go to Judd Street, mix the drinks, plant stuff in the car, dump the blender. She cleaned up the kitchen – not against the law. Convinced, she'll be liberated from conscious guile and may stand a chance. The effective lie, like the masterly golf swing, is free of self-awareness. I've listened to the sports commentaries.

I attend to and sift the descending footsteps. Chief Inspector Allison is light-boned, even bird-like, for all her seniority. There are handshakes. From the sergeant's wooden 'how d'you do' I recognise the older man from yesterday's visit. What's blocked his promotion? Class, education, IQ, scandal – the last, I hope, for which he might take the blame and doesn't need my pity.

The agile chief inspector sits at the kitchen table and invites us all to do the same, as if the house were hers. I imagine my mother thinking that she might more easily mislead a man. Allison spreads a folder, and clicks repeatedly the spring-loaded button of her pen as she speaks. She tells us that the first thing to say – then

170

pauses with great intensity of effect to look, I'm certain, deeply into Trudy and Claude's eyes – is how deeply sorry she is at this loss of a dear husband, dear brother, dear friend. No dear father. I'm fighting a familiar, rising chill of exclusion. But the voice is warm, larger than her frame, relaxed in the burden of office. Her mild cockney is the very register of urban poise and won't be easily challenged. Not by my mother's expensively constrained vowels. No pulling that old trick. History has moved on. One day most British statesmen will speak like the chief inspector. I wonder if she has a gun. Too grand. Like the queen not carrying money. Shooting people is for sergeants and below.

Allison explains that this is an informal conversation to help her form a fuller understanding of the tragic events. Trudy and Claude are under no obligation to answer questions. But she's wrong. They feel they are. To refuse will appear suspicious. But if the chief inspector is one move ahead, she may think that compliance is even more suspect. Those with nothing to hide would insist on a lawyer as a precaution against police error or unlawful intrusion.

As we settle round the table I note and resent the absence of polite queries about me. When's it due? Boy or girl?

Instead, the chief inspector wastes no time. 'You might show me around when we're done talking.'

More statement than request. Claude is eager, too eager, to comply. 'Oh yes. Yes!'

A search warrant would be the alternative. But there's nothing upstairs of interest to the police beyond the squalor.

The chief inspector says to Trudy, 'Your husband came here yesterday about 10 a.m.?'

'That's right.' Her tone is impassive, an example to Claude.

'And there was tension.'

'Of course.'

'Why of course?'

'I've been living with his brother in what John thought was his house.'

'Whose house is it?'

'It's the marital home.'

'The marriage was over?'

'Yes.'

'Mind if I ask? Did he think it was over?'

Trudy hesitates. There may be a right and wrong answer.

'He wanted me back but he wanted his women friends.'

'Know any names?'

'No.'

'But he told you about them.'

'No.'

'But you knew somehow.'

'Of course I *knew*.'

Trudy allows herself a little contempt. As if to say, I'm the real woman here. But she's ignored Claude's coaching. She was to speak the truth, adding and subtracting only what was agreed. I hear my uncle stir in his chair.

Without pause, Allison changes the subject. 'You had a coffee.'

'Yes.

'All three. Round this table?'

'All three.' This is Claude, worried perhaps that his silence is giving a poor impression.

'Anything else?'

'What?'

'With the coffee. Did you offer him anything else?

'No.' My mother sounds cautious.

'And what was in the coffee?'

'Excuse me?'

'Milk? Sugar?'

'He always had it black.' Her pulse rate has risen.

But Clare Allison's manner is impenetrably neutral. She turns to Claude. 'So you lent him money.'

'Yes.'

'How much?'

'Five thousand.' Claude and Trudy answer in ragged chorus.

'A cheque?'

'Cash, actually. It's how he wanted it.'

'Have you been to this juice bar on Judd Street?'

Claude's answer is as quick as the question. 'Once or twice. It was John who told us about it.'

'You weren't there yesterday, I suppose.'

'No.'

'You never borrowed his black hat with the wide brim?'

'Never. Not my sort of thing.'

This may be the wrong answer, but there's not time to work it out. The questions have acquired new weight. Trudy's heart is beating faster. I wouldn't trust her to speak. But she does, in a constricted voice.

'Birthday present from me. He loved that hat.'

The chief inspector is already moving on to something different, but she turns back. 'It's all we can see of him on the CCTV. Sent it off for a DNA match.'

'We haven't offered you any tea or coffee,' Trudy says in her altered voice.

The chief inspector must have refused both for herself and the still-silent sergeant with a shake of the head. 'That's most of it these days,' she says in a tone of nostalgia. 'Science and computer screens. Now, where was – ah yes. There was tension. But I see in the notes there was a row.'

Claude will be making the same racing calculations

as me. His own hair will be found in the hat. The correct answer was yes, he borrowed it a while ago.

'Yes,' Trudy says. 'One of many.'

'Would you mind telling me the—'

'He wanted me to move out. I said I'd go in my own time.'

'When he drove off what was his state of mind?'

'Not good. He was a mess. Confused. He didn't really want me to go. He wanted me back. Tried to make me jealous, pretending that Elodie was his lover. She put us right. There was no affair.'

Too much detail. She's trying to regain control. But talking too fast. She needs to take a breath.

Clare Allison is silent while we wait to know the next direction she'll take. But she stays with this and puts the matter as delicately as she can. 'That's not my information.'

A moment of numbness, as if sound itself has been murdered. The space around me shrinks as Trudy seems to deflate. Her spine slumps like an old woman's. I'm just a little proud of myself. I always had my suspicions. How eagerly they believed Elodie. Now they know: nurse's flowers will certainly not last. But I should be cautious too. The chief inspector might have her own reason to lie. She's clicking her ballpoint pen, ready to move on.

My mother says in a small voice, 'Well, I suppose I was the more deceived.'

'I'm sorry, Mrs Cairncross. But my sources are good. Let's just say that this is a complicated young woman.'

I could explore the theory that it's no bad thing for Trudy to be the injured party, to have corroboration for the story of her faithless husband. But I'm stunned; we're both stunned. My father, that uncertain principle, spins yet further away from me just as the chief inspector comes at my mother with another question. She answers in the same small voice, with the added tremor of a punished little girl.

'Any violence?'

'No.'

'Threats?'

'No.'

'None from you.'

'No.'

'What about his depression? What can you tell me?'

It's kindly said and must be a trap. But Trudy doesn't pause. Too distraught to coin new lies, too persuaded of her truth, she falls back on all she said before, in the same unlikely language. Constant mental pain . . . lashed out at those he loved . . . wrenched the poems from his soul. A vivid image comes to me of a parade of exhausted soldiers with ruined plumage. A sepia memory of a podcast, the Napoleonic Wars in many episodes. Back when my mother and I were at ease. Oh, that Boney had stayed within his borders, I remember thinking, and gone on writing good laws for France.

Claude joins in. 'His own worst enemy.'

The altered acoustic tells me that the chief inspector has turned to look directly at him. 'Any other enemies, apart from himself?'

The tone is unassuming. At best, the form of the question's light-hearted, at worst, fertile with sinister intent.

'I wouldn't know. We were never close.'

'Tell me,' she says, her voice now warmer. 'About your childhood together. That is, if you want to.'

He does. 'I was younger by three years. He was good at everything. Sports, studying, girls. He thought I was an insignificant scab. When I grew up I did the only thing he couldn't. Make money.'

'Property.'

'That sort of thing.'

The chief inspector turns back to Trudy. 'Is this house for sale?'

'Certainly not.'

'I'd heard it was.'

Trudy doesn't respond. Her first good move in several minutes.

I'm wondering if the chief inspector is in uniform. She must be. Her peaked hat will be by her elbow on the table, like a giant beak. I see her as free of mammalian sympathies, narrow-faced, thin-lipped, tight-buttoned. Surely, her head nods pigeon-like when she walks. The sergeant thinks she's a stickler. Bound for promotion out of his league. She'll fly. Either she's decided for John Cairncross's suicide or she has reason to believe that a late third-term gravid is good cover for a crime. Everything the chief inspector says, the least remark, is open to interpretation. The only power we have is to project. She may, like Claude, be clever or stupid or both at once. We just don't know. Our ignorance is her perfect hand. My guess is that she suspects little, knows nothing. That her superiors are watching. That she must be delicate because this conversation is irregular and could compromise due process. That she'll choose what's appropriate over what's true. That her career is her egg and she'll sit on it, warm it, and wait.

But I've been wrong before.

NINETEEN

W HAT NEXT? CLARE ALLISON wishes to look
   around. A bad idea. But to withdraw permission
now, when, for all we know, things are going badly, will
make them worse. The sergeant goes first up the wooden
stairs, followed by Claude, the chief inspector, then my
mother and me. On the ground floor the chief inspector
says that if we wouldn't mind, she'd like to go to the
top and 'work down'. Trudy doesn't care to climb more
stairs. The others continue up while we go into the
sitting room to sit and think.

I dispatch my light-footed thoughts ahead of them,
first to the library. Plaster dust, a smell of death, but
relative order. The floor above, bedroom and bathroom,
chaos of an intimate kind, the bed itself a tangle of lust
and broken sleep, the floor strewn or piled with Trudy's
discarded clothes, the bathroom likewise with lidless
pots, unguents, and dirty underwear. I wonder what
disorder tells suspicious eyes. It can't be morally neutral.
A contempt for things, for order, cleanliness, must lie
on a spectrum with scorn for laws, values, for life itself.
What is a criminal but a disordered spirit? However,
excessive order in a bedroom might be suspicious too.
The chief inspector, bright-eyed as a robin, will take it

in at a glance and come away. But below the level of conscious thought, disgust might bend her judgement.

There are rooms above the first floor but I've never been so far. I bring my thoughts to ground and, like a dutiful child, attend to my mother's state. Her heart rate has settled. She seems almost calm. Perhaps fatalistic. Her engorged bladder presses against my head. But she can't be troubled to move. She's making her calculations, thinking perhaps of their plan. But she should ask herself where her interests lie. Disassociate from Claude. Land him in it somehow. No point in both doing time. Then she and I could languish here. She won't want to give me away when she's alone in a big house. In which case I promise to forgive her. Or deal with her later.

But there's no time for schemes. I hear them coming back down. They pass by the open sitting-room door on their way to the front entrance. The chief inspector surely can't leave without a respectful goodbye to the bereaved wife. In fact Claude has opened the front door and is showing Allison where his brother was parked, how the car failed to start at first, how, despite the row, they had waved when the engine turned and the car reversed into the road. A lesson in truth-telling.

Then Claude and the police are before us.

'Trudy – may I call you Trudy? Such a terrible time and you've been so helpful. So hospitable. I can't—' The chief inspector breaks off, her attention distracted. 'Were these your husband's?'

She's looking at the cardboard boxes my father carried in and left under the bay window. My mother gets to her feet. If there's to be trouble she'd better use her height. And width.

'He was moving back in. Leaving Shoreditch.'

'May I see?'

'Just books. But go ahead.'

There's a gasp from the sergeant as he goes down on his knees to open the boxes. I'd say the chief inspector is squatting on her haunches, not a robin now, but a giant duck. It's wrong of me to dislike her. She's the rule of law and I count myself already in the court of Hobbes. The state must have its monopoly of violence. But the chief inspector's manner irritates me, the way she riffles through my father's possessions, his favourite books, while seeming to talk to herself, knowing we've no choice but to listen.

'Beats me. Very, very sad . . . right on the slip road . . .'

Of course, this is a performance, a prelude. And sure enough. She stands. I think she's looking at Trudy. Perhaps at me.

'But the real mystery is this. Not a single print on that glycol bottle. Nothing on the cup. Just heard from forensics. Not a trace. So strange.'

'Ah!' says Claude, but Trudy cuts across him. I

should warn her. She mustn't be too eager. Her explanation comes out too fast. 'Gloves. Skin complaint. He was so ashamed of his hands.'

'Ah, the gloves!' the chief inspector exclaims. 'You're right. Clean forgot!' She's unfolding a sheet of paper. 'These?'

My mother steps forward to look. It must be a printout of a photograph. 'Yes.'

'Didn't have another pair?'

'Not like these. I used to tell him he didn't need them. No one really minded.'

'Wore them all the time?'

'No. But a lot, especially when he was feeling down.'

The chief inspector is leaving and that's a relief. We're all following her out into the hall.

'Here's a funny thing. Forensics again. Phoned through this morning and it went right out of my mind. Should have told you. So much else going on. Cuts to front-line services. Local crime wave. Anyway. Forefinger and thumb of the right glove. You'd never guess. A nest of tiny spiders. Scores of them. And Trudy, you'll be pleased to know this – babies all doing well. Crawling already!'

The front door is opened, probably by the sergeant. The chief inspector steps outside. As she walks away her voice recedes and merges with the sound of passing traffic. 'Can't for the life of me remember the Latin name. Long time since a hand was in that glove.'

The sergeant lays a hand on my mother's arm and speaks at last, saying softly in parting, 'Back tomorrow morning. Clear up a last few things.'

TWENTY

A T LAST THE MOMENT is on us. There are decisions
to take, urgent, irreversible, self-damning. But first,
Trudy needs two minutes of solitude. We hurry down
to the basement, to the facility the humorous Scots call
the cludgie. There, as the pressure on my skull is relieved
and my mother squats some seconds longer than is neces-
sary, sighing to herself, my thoughts clarify. Or take a
new direction. I thought the murderers should escape,
for the sake of my liberty. This may be too narrow a
view, too self-interested. There are other considerations.
Hatred of my uncle may exceed love for my mother.
Punishing him may be nobler than saving her. But it
might be possible to achieve both.

These concerns remain with me as we return to the
kitchen. It appears that after the police left, Claude
discovered that he needed a Scotch. Hearing it poured
from the bottle as we enter, a seductive sound, Trudy
finds she needs one too. A big one. With tap water, half
and half. Silently, my uncle complies. Silently, they stand
facing each other by the sink. Not the moment for toasts.
They're contemplating each other's errors, or even their
own. Or deciding what to do. This is the emergency
they dreaded and planned for. They knock back their

measures and without speaking settle for another. Our lives are about to change. Chief Inspector Allison looms above us, a capricious, smiling god. We won't know, until it's too late, why she didn't make the arrests just then, why she's left us alone. Rolling up the case, waiting for the DNA on the hat, moving on? Mother and uncle must consider that any choice they make now could be just the one she has in mind for them, and she's waiting. Just as possible, this, their mysterious plan, won't have occurred to her and they could be one step ahead. One good reason to act boldly. Instead, for now, they prefer a drink. Perhaps whatever they do obliges Clare Allison, including an interlude with a single malt. But no, their only chance is to make the radical choice – and now.

Trudy raises an arm to forestall a third. Claude is more steadfast. He's in strict pursuit of mental clarity. We listen to him pour – he's having it neat, and long – then we listen to him swallow hard, that familiar sound. They might be wondering how they can avoid a row just when they need a common purpose. From far away comes the sound of a siren, an ambulance, merely, but it speaks to their fears. The latticework of the state lies invisibly across the city. Hard to escape it. It's a prompt, for at last, there's speech, a useful statement of the obvious.

'This is bad.' My mother's voice is croaky and low. 'Where are the passports?'

'I've got them. And the cash?'

'In my case.'

But they don't move and the asymmetry of the exchange – Trudy's evasive reply – doesn't provoke my uncle. He's well into his third as Trudy's first reaches me. Hardly sensual, but it speaks or sinks to the occasion, to a sense of an ending with no beginning in sight. I conjure an old military road through a cold glen, a whiff of wet stone and peat, the sound of steel and patient trudging on loose rock, and the weight of bitter injustice. So far from the south-facing slopes, the dusty bloom on swelling purple clusters framing receding hills and their overlapping shades of ever paler indigo. I'd rather be there. But I'm conceding – the Scotch, my first, sets something free. A harsh liberation – the open gate leads to struggle and fear of what the mind might devise. It's happening now to me. I'm asked, I'm asking myself, what it is that I most want now. Anything I want. Realism not a limiting factor. Cut the ropes, set the mind free. I can answer without thinking – I'm going through the open gate.

Footsteps on the stairs. Trudy and Claude look up, startled. Has the inspector found a way into the house? Has a burglar chosen the worst of all nights? This is a slow, heavy descent. They see black leather shoes, then a belted waist, a shirt stained with vomit, then a terrible expression, both blank and purposeful.

My father wears the clothes he died in. His face is bloodless, the already rotting lips are greenish-black, the eyes, tiny and penetrating. Now he stands at the foot of the stairs, taller than we remember him. He's come from the mortuary to find us and knows exactly what he wants. I'm shaking because my mother is. There's no shimmer, nothing ghostly. It's not an hallucination. This is my corporeal father, John Cairncross, exactly as he is. My mother's moan of fear acts as an enticement, for he's walking towards us.

'John,' Claude says warily, on a rising note, as if he could wake this figure into proper non-existence. 'John, it's us.'

This seems well understood. He stands close before us, exuding a sweet miasma of glycol and maggot-friendly flesh. It's my mother he stares at with small, hard, black eyes made of imperishable stone. His disgusting lips move but he makes no sound. The tongue is blacker than the lips. Fixing his gaze on her all the while, he stretches out an arm. His fleshless hand fastens on my uncle's throat. My mother can't even scream. Still, the illiquid eyes remain on her. This is for her, his gift. The remorseless, one-handed grip tightens. Claude drops to his knees, his eyes are bulging, his hands beat and pull uselessly at his brother's arm. Only a distant squeaking, the piteous sound of a mouse, tells us that he's still alive. Then he isn't. My father, who hasn't glanced at him once, lets him drop, and now draws his wife to him, enfolds her in arms that are thin and strong, like steel rods. He pulls her face towards his and kisses her long and hard with icy, putrefying lips. Terror and disgust and shame overwhelm her. The moment will torment her until she dies. Indifferently, he releases her, and walks back the way he came. Even as he climbs the stairs he begins to fade.

Well, I was asked. I asked myself. And that's what I wanted. A childish Halloween fantasy. How else to commission a spirit revenge in a secular age? The Gothic has been reasonably banished, the witches have fled the heath, and materialism, so troubling to the soul, is all I have left. A voice on the radio once told me that when we fully understand what matter is we'll feel better. I doubt that. I'll never get what I want.

* * *

I emerge from reveries to find us in the bedroom. I've no memory of the ascent. The hollow sound of the wardrobe door, a clank of coat hangers, a suitcase lifted onto the bed, and another, then a brisk snap of locks opening. They should have packed in readiness. The inspector might even come tonight. Are they calling this a plan? I hear curses and muttering.

'Where is it? I had it here. In my hand!'

They criss-cross the bedroom, open drawers, move in and out of the bathroom. Trudy drops a glass that shatters on the floor. She hardly cares. For some reason, the radio is on. Claude sits with his laptop and mumbles, 'Train's at nine. Taxi's on its way.'

I'd prefer Paris to Brussels. Better onward connections. Trudy, still in the bathroom, mutters to herself, 'Dollars . . . euros.'

Everything they say, even the sounds they make, have an air of valediction, like a sadly resolving chord, a sung farewell. This is the end; we aren't coming back. The house, my grandfather's house I should have grown up in, is about to fade. I won't remember it. I'd like to summon a list of countries without extradition treaties. Most are uncomfortable, unruly, hot. I've heard that Beijing is a pleasant spot for runaways. A thriving village of English-speaking villains buried deep in the populated vastness of a world city. A fine place to end up.

'Sleeping pills, painkillers,' Claude calls out.

His voice, its tone, prompts me. Time to decide. He's closing up the cases, fastening leather straps. So quick. They must have been half-packed already. These are old-fashioned two-wheeled items, not four. Claude lifts them to the floor.

Trudy says, 'Which?'

I think she's holding up two scarves. Claude grunts his choice. This is only a pretence of normality. When they board the train, when they cross the border, their guilt will declare itself. They only have an hour and they should hurry. Trudy says there's a coat she wants and can't find. Claude insists she won't need it.

'It's lightweight,' she says. 'The white one.'

'You'll stand out in a crowd. On CCTV.'

But she finds it anyway, just as Big Ben strikes eight and the news comes on. They don't pause to listen. There are still last things to gather up. In Nigeria, children burned alive in front of their parents by keepers of the flame. In North Korea, a rocket is launched. Worldwide, rising sea levels run ahead of predictions. But none of these is first. That's reserved for a new catastrophe. A combination, poverty and war, with climate change held in reserve, driving millions from their homes, an ancient epic in new form, vast movements of people, like engorged rivers in spring, Danubes, Rhines and Rhones of angry or desolate or hopeful people, crammed at borders against the razor-wire gates, drowning in thousands to share in the fortunes of the West. If, as the new cliché goes, this is biblical, the seas are not parting for them, not the Aegean, not the English Channel. Old Europa tosses in her dreams, she pitches between pity and fear, between helping and repelling. Emotional and kind this week, scaly-hearted and so reasonable the next, she wants to help but she doesn't want to share or lose what she has.

And always, there are problems closer at hand. As

radios and TVs everywhere drone on, people continue about their business. A couple has finished packing for a journey. The cases are closed, but there's a picture of her mother that the young woman wants to bring. The heavy carved frame is too large to pack. Without the right tool the photograph can't be removed, and the tool, a special kind of key, is in the basement, deep in a drawer. A taxi waits outside. The train leaves in fifty-five minutes, the station is a good way off, there may be queues for security and passport control. The man carries a suitcase out to the landing and returns, a little out of breath. He should have made use of the wheels.

'We absolutely have to go.'

'I've got to have this picture.'

'Carry it under your arm.'

But she has a handbag, her white coat, a suitcase to tow, and me to carry.

With a moan, Claude lifts the second suitcase to carry it out. By this unneeded effort he's making a point about urgency.

'It won't take you a minute. It's in a front corner of the left-hand drawer.'

He returns. 'Trudy. We're leaving. Now.'

The exchange has grown from terse to bitter.

'You carry it for me.'

'Out of the question.'

'Claude. It's my mother.'

'I don't care. We're leaving.'

But they're not. After all my turns and revisions, misinterpretations, lapses of insight, attempts at self-annihilation, and sorrow in passivity, I've come to a decision. Enough. My amniotic sac is the translucent silk purse, fine and strong, that contains me. It also holds the fluid that protects me from the world and its bad dreams. No longer. Time to join in. To end the endings. Time to begin. It's not easy to free my right arm lodged tight against my chest, or gain movement in my wrist. But now it's done. A forefinger is my own special tool to remove *my* mother from the frame. Two weeks early and finger-nails so long. I make my first attempt at an incision. My nails are soft and, however fine, the fabric is tough. Evolution knows its business. I feel for the indent my finger made. There's a crease, well defined, and that's where I try again, and again, until the fifth attempt, when I feel the faintest rendering, and on the sixth, the tiniest rupture. Into this tear I succeed in working the tip of my nail, my finger, then two fingers, three, four, and at last my balled fist punches through and there follows behind it a great outpouring, the cataract at the beginning of life. My watery protection has vanished.

Now I'll never know how the business of the photo-graph or the nine o'clock train would have been resolved. Claude is outside the room at the head of the stairs. He'll have a case in each hand, ready to descend.

My mother calls out with what sounds like a disappointed moan. 'Oh Claude.'

'What now?'

'My waters. Breaking!'

'We'll deal with it later. On the train.'

He must believe it's a ploy, a continuation of the argument, a repellent form of womanly trouble that he's too frantic to consider.

I'm shrugging off the caul, my first experience of undressing. I'm clumsy. Three dimensions seem three too many. I foresee the material world will be a challenge. My discarded shroud remains twisted round my knees. No matter. I've new business below my head. I don't know how I know what to do. It's a mystery. There's some knowledge we simply arrive with. In my case, there's this, and a smattering of poetic scansion. No blank slate after all. I bring that same hand to my cheek, and slide further along the muscular wall of the uterus to reach down and find the cervix. It's a tight squeeze against the back of my head. It's there, at the opening to the world, that I delicately palpate with puny fingers and immediately, as if some spell has been uttered, the great power of my mother is provoked, the walls around me ripple then tremble and close in on me. It's an earthquake, it's a giant stirring in her cave. Like the sorcerer's apprentice, I'm horrified then crushed by the strength that's unleashed. I should have waited my turn. Only a fool would mess with such force. From far away I hear my mother call out. It could be a shout for help or a scream of triumph or pain. And then I feel it on the top of my head, my crown – one centimetre dilated! No turning back.

Trudy has crawled onto the bed. Claude is somewhere near the door. She's panting, excited, and very afraid.

'It's started. It's so quick! Get an ambulance.'

He says nothing for a moment, then he asks simply, 'Where's my passport?'

The failure is mine. I underestimated him. The point in arriving early was to ruin Claude. I knew he was trouble. But I thought he loved my mother and would stay with her. I'm beginning to understand her fortitude. Over the bright jingling sound of coins against mascara case as he rummages through her handbag, she says, 'I hid it. Downstairs. Just in case this happened.'

He considers. He's dealt in property, he owned a skyscraper in Cardiff and knows about a deal. 'Tell me where it is and I'll call you an ambulance. Then I'll go.'

Her voice is cautious. Closely observing her own state, waiting for, wanting and dreading the next wave. 'No. If I'm going down so are you.'

'Fine. No ambulance.'

'I'll call them myself. As soon—'

As soon as the second contraction, stronger than the first, has passed. Again, her involuntary shout, and the whole body clenching as Claude crosses the room to the bed, to the locker at its side, to disconnect the phone, while I'm violently compressed, and lifted, sucked down and backwards an inch or two from my resting place. An iron band around my head is tightening. Our three fates are being crushed in one maw.

As the wave recedes, Claude, like a border official, says dully, 'Passport?'

She shakes her head, waits to get her breath. They hold each other in a form of equilibrium.

She recovers and says in a level voice, 'Then you'll have to be the midwife.'

'Not my baby.'

'It's never the midwife's baby.'

She's frightened, but she can terrify him with instructions.

'When it comes out it'll be face down. You'll pick it up, both hands, very gently, supporting the head and place it on me. Still face down, between my breasts. Near my heartbeat. Don't worry about the cord. It'll stop beating on its own and the baby will start to breathe. You'll put a couple of towels over it to keep it warm. Then we wait.'

'Wait? Christ. For what?'

'For the placenta to be born.'

If he flinched or retched, I don't know. His calculation might still be that we could get this over with and catch a later train.

I listen closely, intent on learning what to do. Duck under a towel. Breathe. Don't say a word. But *it*! Surely, pink or blue!

'So go and get a pile of towels. It'll be messy. Scrub your hands with the nailbrush and lots of soap.'

So far out of his depth, so far from a friendly shore, a man without his papers who should be on the run. He turns to go and do what he's told.

So it continues, wave on wave, shouts and wails, and pleas for the agony to cease. Unmerciful progress, relentless ejection. The cord unreels behind me as I make my slow way forward. Forward and out. Pitiless forces of nature intend to flatten me. I travel a section where I know a portion of my uncle has passed too often the other way. I'm not troubled. What was in his day a vagina, is now proudly a birth canal, my Panama, and I'm greater than he was, a stately ship of genes, dignified by unhurried progress, freighted with my cargo of ancient information. No casual cock can compete. For a stretch, I'm deaf, blind and dumb, it hurts everywhere. But it pains my screaming mother more as she renders the sacrifice all mothers make for their big-headed, loud-mouthed infants.

A slithering moment of waxy, creaking emergence, and here I am, set naked on the kingdom. Like stout Cortez (I remember a poem my father once recited), I'm amazed. I'm looking down, with what wonder and surmise, at the napped surface of a blue bath towel. Blue. I've always known, verbally at least, I've always been able to infer what's blue – sea, sky, lapis lazuli, gentians – mere abstractions. Now I have it at last, I own it, and it possesses me. More gorgeous than I dared believe. That's just a beginning, at the indigo end of the spectrum.

My faithful cord, the lifeline that failed to kill me, suddenly dies its allotted death. I'm breathing. Delicious. My advice to newborns: don't cry, look around, taste the air. I'm in London. The air is good. Sounds are crisp, brilliant with the treble turned up. The lambent towel beaming its colour summons the Goharshad mosque in Iran that made my father cry at dawn. My mother stirs and causes my head to turn. I have a glimpse of Claude. Smaller than I cast him, with narrow shoulders and a foxy look. No mistaking an expression of disgust. Evening sunlight through a plane tree throws a stirring pattern on the ceiling. Ah, the joy of straightening my legs, of noting from the alarm clock on the bedside table that they'll never make their train. But I don't have long to savour the moment. My pliant ribcage is clamped by the squeamish hands of a killer and I'm placed on the snowy-soft welcoming belly of another.

Her heartbeat is distant, muffled, but familiar, like an old chorus not heard in half a lifetime. The music's marking is andante, a delicate footfall leading me to the true open gate. I can't deny the dread I feel. But I'm dead beat, a shipwrecked sailor on a lucky beach. I'm falling, even as the ocean licks around my ankles.

* * *

Trudy and I must have dozed. I don't know how many minutes have passed until we hear the doorbell. How clear it sounds. Claude is still here, still hoping for his passport. He may have been downstairs to hunt. Now he goes towards the videophone. He glances at the screen and turns away. There can be no surprises.

'Four of them,' he says, more to himself.

We contemplate this. It's over. It's not a good end. It was never going to be.

My mother moves me so we can exchange a long look. The moment I've waited for. My father was right, it is a lovely face. The hair darker than I thought, the eyes a paler green, the cheeks still flushed with recent effort, the nose indeed a tiny thing. I think I see the entire world in this face. Beautiful. Loving. Murderous. I hear Claude cross the room with resigned tread to go downstairs. No ready phrase. Even in this moment of repose, during this long, greedy stare into my mother's eyes, I'm thinking about the taxi waiting outside. A waste. Time to send it away. And I'm thinking about our prison cell – I hope it's not too small – and beyond its heavy door, worn steps ascending: first sorrow, then justice, then meaning. The rest is chaos.

penguin.co.uk/vintage